Sabrina took a deep breath and walked to center stage.

Out of forty-three starters, she was one of two contestants left in the Other Realm Annual Spelling Bee for newly licensed card-carrying witches. If she didn't cast a working fountain-of-truth spell, she'd be out of the round and the competition.

A tense hush settled over the audience seated in the amphitheater on the summit of Cloud Nine Mountain when Sabrina turned to face them.

Aunt Hilda and Aunt Zelda sat in the front row, their smiles fixed around gritted teeth, their fingers crossed.

Salem lounged in the seat between them. "Why don't they ever ask them to cast a turn-the-cat-back-into-a-warlock spell?"

"To keep the world safe from maniacal monarchs out to corner the global tuna market," Zelda said, scowling the cat into silence.

Why do I let my aunts talk me into these things? Sabrina looked away from her guardians as she limbered up her pointing finger with a few knuckle bends. *It's just a spelling bee! How much damage can losing do to the Spellman family honor?*

"What's the matter, Sabrina?" Agatha MacFadden's sarcastic tone sliced through the quiet. "Nervous?"

Sabrina, the Teenage Witch® books

Available from ARCHWAY Paperbacks

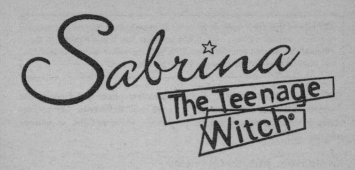

Sabrina The Teenage Witch®

Reality Check

Diana G. Gallagher

Based upon the characters in Archie Comics

And based upon the television series
Sabrina, The Teenage Witch
Created for television by Nell Scovell
Developed for television by Jonathan Schmock

AN ARCHWAY PAPERBACK
Published by POCKET BOOKS
New York   London   Toronto   Sydney   Singapore

This book is a work of fiction. Names, characters, places and incidents are products of the author's imagination or are used fictitiously. Any resemblance to actual events or locales or persons, living or dead, is entirely coincidental.

AN ARCHWAY PAPERBACK *Original*

An Archway Paperback published by
POCKET BOOKS, a division of Simon & Schuster Inc.
1230 Avenue of the Americas, New York, NY 10020

ISBN: 0-671-04069-3

First Archway Paperback printing July 2000

10 9 8 7 6 5 4 3 2 1

AN ARCHWAY PAPERBACK and colophon are registered trademarks of Simon & Schuster Inc.

SABRINA THE TEENAGE WITCH and all related titles, logos and characters are trademarks of Archie Comics Publications, Inc.

Printed in the U.S.A.

IL: 4+

For Amber and Monica, best friends

Reality Check

Chapter 1

Sabrina took a deep breath and walked to center stage. Out of forty-three starters, she was one of two contestants left in the Other Realm Annual Spelling Bee for newly licensed card-carrying witches. If she didn't cast a working fountain-of-truth spell, she'd be out of the round and the competition.

Unless Agatha MacFadden's next spell fails too, Sabrina thought. *Which isn't likely.* Agatha was arrogant and extremely annoying, but she had done her witch work.

A tense hush settled over the audience seated in the amphitheater on the summit of Cloud Nine Mountain when Sabrina turned to face them.

Aunt Hilda and Aunt Zelda sat in the front row, their smiles fixed around gritted teeth, their fingers crossed.

Salem lounged in the seat between them. "Why don't they ever ask them to cast a turn-the-cat-back-into-a-warlock spell?"

"To keep the world safe from maniacal monarchs out to corner the global tuna market," Zelda said, scowling the cat into silence.

Why do I let my aunts talk me into these things? Sabrina looked away from her guardians as she limbered up her pointing finger with a few knuckle bends. *It's just a spelling bee! How much damage can losing do to the Spellman family honor?*

"What's the matter, Sabrina?" Agatha MacFadden's sarcastic tone sliced through the quiet. "Nervous?"

Like I'm not under enough pressure! Sabrina's anxiety intensified as she turned to stare at the smug young witch waiting on the sidelines. Condescending conceit was obviously a MacFadden family trait.

Agatha's aunts, Florence and Charlene, were the leverage Hilda and Zelda had used to convince Sabrina to participate in the traditional spectacle of dueling spells. Both Spellman sisters had lost to a MacFadden when they had competed in the Spelling Bee after getting their licenses centuries before. As a rule, Hilda and Zelda would have accepted defeat graciously and forgotten about it—except the MacFaddens wouldn't let them forget. Florence and Charlene took every opportunity to remind them—and everyone else within earshot at

Other Realm gatherings—that they had been and always would be superior witches.

"Just warming up," Sabrina retorted, smiling.

Agatha rolled brilliant blue eyes and flipped her long, dark hair over her shoulder. Tastefully clothed in designer velour, denim, and leather, with a trim figure and flawless cameo complexion, she looked like a porcelain doll.

With the personality of a sadistic lemon, Sabrina thought wryly.

"Whenever you're ready, Sabrina." Drell frowned from his seat at the judges' table. "Preferably before the end of the *next* millennium."

Agatha smirked.

"Right. One truth spell coming up." Sabrina graced the judges with a tight smile, then scanned the audience.

By attending the event, spectators volunteered to be subjects of spells that required them. None of the contestants' spells were sealed, but they remained in effect until someone won—whether the magic worked properly or not. At the moment, the audience contained a giant toadstool, a witch with smoking ears, and something that resembled a dehydrated swamp creature. Fortunately, the contestants were also exempt from any responsibility regarding spells gone awry.

Sabrina raised her finger to randomly select a subject for the fountain-of-truth spell.

"Take your time, Sabrina!" Florence MacFadden, a thin woman with straight brown hair and beady eyes set in a pinched face, chuckled softly and nudged her sister.

"You're not the first Spellman to suffer from stage fright, dear." Shorter and rounder than Florence, Charlene MacFadden glanced down the front row at Hilda.

Hilda stiffened and glared back. "I did *not* have stage fright! You put a mute-and-freeze hex on me, Charlene!"

"That's *still* a lame excuse, Hilda." Charlene sighed and fluffed her curly red hair.

Eyes flashing, Hilda raised her finger.

Shaking her head, Zelda grabbed Hilda's hand.

Determination replaced Sabrina's nervous jitters. In Aunt Hilda's final Spelling Bee round with Charlene, she had suddenly become too petrified and choked up to speak. Aunt Zelda had lost to Florence when she'd become tongue-tied and none of her words had made sense. Charlene had just confessed to cheating, and Sabrina suspected Florence had used the same underhanded tactics on Zelda.

Avenging the Spellman family honor suddenly seemed like a dynamite idea. Sabrina's finger flexed, poised to strike.

"Powered by the magic mountain,
truth flows from the hanging fountain."

Sabrina snapped a point at Charlene, and a small, ornately carved mini-fountain appeared above the witch's head.

The startled witch squealed as sparkling bursts of light overflowed the fountain bowl and fell on her head and shoulders. "No fair!"

"Foul!" Florence brushed sparkles off her shoulder, then leaned back out of range.

Hilda grinned. "All's fair in love, war, and the Spelling Bee, Charlene. I've heard you say it a hundred times."

"At least," Zelda nodded.

With a thoughtful frown, Sabrina paused, then raised her finger to complete the spell.

"In your zeal my aunt to beat,
did you, Charlene MacFadden, cheat?"

Sabrina pointed at Charlene again and breathlessly awaited the result.

"Of course I cheated!" Charlene's eyes bulged as the truth poured out of her mouth. "It was the only way I could win!"

"Yes!" Hilda jumped out of her seat. "Vindicated after all these years!"

"Hey!" Salem perked up. "Since Charlene won't be gloating about beating Hilda anymore, can we go to the Other Realm All-You-Can-Eat Clambake this year?"

"I don't know, Salem," Zelda frowned. "I'd still have to listen to Florence brag about beating me."

"Not if you wear earplugs," Salem suggested.

Sabrina glanced toward the judges' table as Drell and the other witches on the panel conferred.

After several long seconds, Drell stood up. He looked magnificently ridiculous in his flowing wizard robes and pointed hat, which he only wore on rare, but highly prestigious, occasions. He paused for dramatic effect, then boomed, "Pass!"

Thunderous applause and cheers filled the theater as Sabrina returned to her side of the stage and Agatha stepped forward. The competition would continue until one of them won a round.

Drell reached into a ceremonial cauldron on the table and pulled out a folded paper. He opened it, cleared his throat, then announced, "A spying eye spell."

A murmur of anticipation rippled through the audience.

Sabrina felt a rush of elation. Spy spells were tricky and subject to strange interpretations if the incantation wasn't worded exactly right. She crossed her fingers. A Spellman victory might be only one bad rhyme away.

Agatha breathed in deeply and focused—on Salem!

"Cloak and dagger, seek and hide,
be my spying ears and eyes!"

"What?" Salem cringed as Agatha's finger zapped him. He immediately began to fade.

Within seconds he was invisible except for his eyes, ears, and a huge, toothy grin with a brilliant *ping!*

"No offense, Salem, but I don't think that's a winning smile," Hilda said.

Sabrina tensed as the judges put their heads together. Since the spell would be reversed once the contest ended, she wasn't worried about Salem. She just wanted the competition to end so she could get back to her mortal life in Westbridge.

But I want to go home a winner! Sabrina had resented the unintended pressure her aunts had put on her to enter the Spelling Bee and restore the family's reputation, but now that she had met the Mac-Faddens, she was just as anxious for a Spellman victory as they were.

When Drell rose again, everyone leaned forward expectantly. "After due consideration, the judges unanimously rule that a *pinging* grin is hardly appropriate in an effective surreptitious surveillance spell."

"A what spell?" Florence asked, puzzled.

"An undercover spying spell that works," Zelda quietly explained.

Drell scowled at the whispering witches, then continued. "Therefore, Agatha MacFadden's spell fails, and Sabrina Spellman is declared this year's winner!"

"Wahoo!" Sabrina raised victorious fists and jumped with joy.

More cheers and whistles erupted from the audience.

"I'd giggle with glee, but my teeth seem to be stuck," Salem muttered. He slowly returned to normal along with the other subjects as the effects of the contest spells wore off.

Hilda and Zelda grabbed each other and laughed. "She won! She won!"

Agatha glowered at Sabrina, then stalked into the wings.

Florence and Charlene sat in frozen, dumbstruck disbelief.

Drell picked up an envelope and motioned Sabrina to join him in the center of the stage.

"Gosh, I hope it's a gift certificate to WitchWare on-line," Hilda said. "We could upgrade the laptop."

"Good idea!" Zelda grinned, then became more subdued. "But it's Sabrina's prize and she can use whatever it is for whatever she wants."

"Like keeping the adorable family cat in caviar and fresh shrimp for the next six months," Salem sighed.

Sabrina hurried to join the head of the Witches' Council in the spotlight. She had tried hard to win so the MacFaddens would stop taunting her aunts. She hadn't thought about actually winning *something*. But since first prize might be a lifetime subscription to *Other Realm Geographic* or a shopping spree at Novelty Potions and Spells, she kept a lid on her excitement.

"Congratulations, Sabrina." Drell smiled like he actually meant it. "As this year's winner your name will, of course, be engraved on the permanent plaque at the base of the mountain."

"Cool!" Sabrina tried to look suitably impressed. "What did I win?"

"Oh, yes." Drell pushed a lock of hair back under his hat. "And I'm pleased to present you with"—Sabrina held her breath as Drell opened the envelope—"a reality check!" Drell waved a small, imprinted paper, then gave it to Sabrina.

The audience oohed and ahhed.

"That should have been mine!" Furious, Agatha stormed offstage and ran to her aunts.

"Don't worry, Agatha." Florence put a comforting arm around the pouting girl's shoulders, then turned to her sister. "We'll get even."

Charlene's flaming red curls bounced as she nodded. "Soon."

Sabrina stared at the check as her name appeared on the Payable To line in gleaming gold script. There weren't any spaces for a cash value. "What is *this?*"

"A reality check. *Don't* ask me to say it again." Shaking his head, Drell pulled off his pointed wizard hat and left as the house lights came up.

"I don't *need* to check my reality! I live in the mortal world with a talking cat and two eccentric witches!"

Drell just kept walking.

"You're a big help," Sabrina muttered. Her aunts and Salem rushed toward her as she hopped off the stage.

"You were great, Sabrina!" Hilda took the check from her niece's hand. "And this is fantastic! I don't think they've ever awarded a reality check before."

"We should probably put it in the safe deposit box and save it for an emergency," Zelda said.

"I think she should cash it in now," Salem purred. "I'm sure we can figure out exactly what point in time the Other Realm cops figured out I was trying to take over the world. With a little more security, I would have gotten away with it. Then I wouldn't be a cat."

"Wait a minute." Sabrina looked from one aunt to the other. "I'm obviously out of the loop here. What exactly *is* a reality check?"

"Very rare." Hilda handed the check back with a wistful sigh. "The Witches' Council is the only institution with the power to issue them, and they don't do it very often."

"That didn't answer my question," Sabrina said. "What can *I* do with it?"

"After you endorse it, you can cash it in to change *one* instance of reality without any dire repercussions." Zelda smiled, but her tone was grave.

"What's the catch?" Sabrina asked. She had been a witch long enough to know that anything magical that seemed too good to be true usually was. She was certain the reality check was no exception.

"No catch," Zelda assured her. "That's why I think you should save it for an unexpected disaster."

"*She* shouldn't have it at all!" Florence marched forward, flanked by Charlene and Agatha.

"Sabrina won fair and square," Zelda huffed.

"Which is more than *you* can say!" Hilda fixed Charlene with a scathing scowl.

"So now we're even and maybe we can all be friends, right?" Still basking in the glow of victory, Sabrina wasn't in the mood to feud. She looked hopefully at Agatha, but the girl stubbornly folded her arms and frowned.

Charlene planted her hands on her hips to square off with Hilda. "Just because I outsmarted you doesn't mean you're a better witch than I am, Hilda Spellman."

"Oh, yeah?" Hilda's eyes narrowed. "Maybe we should step outside and have this out once and for all."

"No need for that," Florence said.

"Really?" A storm brewed under Zelda's calm exterior. "Then you admit you put a verbal dyslexia spell on me to win the Spelling Bee, Florence?"

"Never!" Florence stiffened.

"I guess a truce isn't an option then?" Sabrina asked, even though no one was listening. She didn't blame Aunt Hilda and Aunt Zelda for being upset, but the confrontation was quickly stripping the luster off her winning glow. "So how about a cold war strategy? You know, where nobody on one side speaks to anyone on the other side."

"Yes, I'm tired of talking." Florence's eyes blazed.

"Me, too!" Charlene rolled up her sleeves.

"So are we." Zelda picked up Salem and took Hilda's arm. "Come on, Sabrina. We're leaving."

As Sabrina turned to follow her aunts, Charlene began an incantation.

> *"Two and four and time to do,*
> *Hilda, now the laugh's on you!"*

Charlene whipped off a point, catching Hilda totally off guard.

Hilda began to giggle.

Florence picked up the chant.

> *"Two and four, not over yet,*
> *here and there she will forget!"*

Zelda flinched when Florence pointed at her.

"Hey!" Sabrina quickly pointed a protective ward around herself when Agatha raised her finger. Her aunts had not been so lucky. Florence and Charlene had blindsided them before they could defend themselves.

Hilda doubled over with hysterical laughter.

Zelda blinked at the cat cradled in her arms. "What a pretty kitty. Are you lost?"

"No," Salem drawled, "I'm right here."

"Aunt Zelda?" When her aunt didn't respond, Sabrina touched her arm. "Hello? Aunt Zelda?"

Hilda collapsed on the floor, still laughing.

"Hmmm?" Zelda looked up at Sabrina, her expression blank. "Do I know you?"

Chapter 2

Oh, boy! Sabrina stared, numb with shock. Aunt Zelda didn't recognize her, and Aunt Hilda was rolling on the floor, laughing so hard she couldn't catch her breath.

"Are you lost?" Aunt Zelda asked Sabrina.

"Lost would seem to be the operative word," Salem said. "As in you've totally lost it."

Zelda frowned at the cat. "Do I know you?"

Think! Sabrina forced herself to remain calm. Living with eccentric aunts who were also witches was one thing. She was not up to coping with eccentric witch aunts who had been turned into an airhead and a hysteric. She briefly considered cashing in the reality check so Zelda and Hilda could counter the MacFaddens' ambush *before* the insidious spells hit. However, since she was convinced

14

there was a catch to the "no dire consequences" clause, she stuffed the check in her pocket and spun around to face the MacFaddens instead.

"Undo whatever you did to them!" Sabrina demanded. "Right now."

"My, aren't *we* testy!" Charlene waved as she flounced off.

"Spoilsport." Florence flicked a casual point over her shoulder as she grabbed on to Agatha and followed Charlene.

Agatha looked back and smiled.

That was way too easy, Sabrina thought uneasily.

"What are you doing on the floor, Hilda?" Zelda asked.

Distracted by her recovering aunts, Sabrina put the vindictive MacFaddens out of her mind. At least their spells had been reversed, although Aunt Zelda apparently had no memory of her memory lapse. On the other hand, Aunt Hilda was very much aware of the MacFaddens' foul play.

"Plotting my revenge against Charlene," Hilda groaned as she got to her feet.

"Stooping to her level won't solve anything. Besides, now that Sabrina's won the Spelling Bee, I don't think they'll be bothering us again." Zelda scratched Salem behind the ears. "Now, let's go."

Most of the crowd had already dispersed, and they didn't have to wait long to catch a feeder tube to the inter-world transit hub. Obnoxious witches and their nasty spells aside, Sabrina decided the day had been a complete success. She had brought honor back to the Spellman name and her name would be permanently inscribed on the Spelling Bee Plaque to prove it.

The reality check would make a nice souvenir of the event. *Framed and hanging on the wall.* Since magic used for personal gain *always* produced dire consequences, she was certain cashing the reality check would have disastrous effects.

Unless—

Sabrina stopped dead in the doorway of the linen closet transit system to the mortal world. *What if the check is already having an effect on reality?* she thought to herself. She *had* considered using it to save her aunts from the MacFaddens' sneaky spell attack!

"Sabrina!" Hilda grabbed her arm and yanked her through the transit portal a split second before she was trapped in the closing doors. "Don't you know what happens if you get caught between worlds?"

Sabrina blinked. "No. What?"

Thunder boomed and lightning flashed.

"Your molecules get scrambled and confused," Zelda said.

"And then you just drift between the Other Realm and the mortal world like a ghost," Hilda added. She opened the linen closet door and stepped out.

Zelda nodded. "Invisible."

"And no one can hear you." Salem shuddered.

"Scream?" Sabrina dashed through the door to the safety of the upstairs hall.

"But it didn't happen." The cat leaped from Zelda's arms onto the wicker basket. "So cheer up!"

"I second that!" Zelda clasped her hands together and smiled. "We should all go out and celebrate Sabrina's victory."

"Or, to put it another way, the MacFaddens' long-overdue defeat." Hilda brightened. "Pizza or Chinese?"

"I know this great sushi place," Salem suggested.

"I'm not going anywhere! Don't you understand what's happening?" Suddenly frantic, Sabrina shifted her gaze between them.

"Besides the fact that you seem to be having a nervous breakdown?" Salem cocked his head.

Hilda placed her hand on Sabrina's forehead. "She doesn't have a fever."

"I'm not sick." Sabrina pulled the reality check out of her pocket and shook it. "It's this!"

"The reality check?" Zelda looked at Hilda and shrugged.

"Did Drell forget to sign it?" Hilda snapped the check from Sabrina's hand. "No, it's signed. So what's the problem?"

"See! Even *you* don't know!" Sabrina grabbed the check and ran into her room. She paused in the doorway and glanced back at her mystified aunts. "But they can't fool me. Not *this* time."

Sabrina closed the door, locked it, then placed the check on her desk and flopped on her bed.

"Sabrina?" Zelda called softly and rapped on the door. "Wouldn't you like to talk about what's bothering you?"

"Maybe later, Aunt Zelda! I'm, uh . . . kind of tired after all that spell casting." Sabrina didn't want to shut her aunts out, but it was for their own good. When calamity struck, they wouldn't be at ground zero.

And she was positive that calamity would strike.

In just the past thirty minutes, the MacFaddens had surprised Hilda and Zelda with humiliating spells and she had almost become a ghost in the Other Realm Twilight Zone. If the MacFaddens hadn't reversed the spells or if Aunt Hilda hadn't pulled her away from the transport doors, she would have endorsed the reality check to make everything okay again.

Only things probably would have gotten worse!

Somehow the check was making bad things happen so she'd *have* to cash it!

The only way to prevent that from happening was to stay put and do nothing.

"What's wrong with her?" Worried and a little irritated, Hilda folded her arms and stared at the closed door. There was no reason Sabrina should be upset about winning a reality check. The next time she got into some seemingly impossible mess, a simple signature would get her out of it.

"I know." Zelda frowned at the door. "Maybe she is just tired. We did make a big deal about how important it was to us to win."

"I guess that would wear on her nerves." Hilda sighed. Sabrina hadn't been interested in participating in the Spelling Bee at all until she and Zelda had begged her to enter because Agatha MacFadden was competing. The event was supposed to be fun. They had turned it into a battleground. Still, Sabrina had risen to the challenge and won the Spelling Bee in spite of the pressure. She had even saved them from Florence and Charlene's spells!

So why doesn't she want to party?

"And the Spelling Bee is pretty intensive," Zelda added. "All that pointing and rhyming can be exhausting."

"Watching all that pointing makes *me* hungry." Salem jumped down from the basket and rubbed against Zelda's leg. "That was a hint."

"All right, Salem." Zelda cast a concerned glance at Sabrina's door as she moved toward the stairs. "Maybe we should just let her rest awhile, Hilda."

"I suppose." Hilda suppressed a twinge of disappointment as she followed Zelda and Salem downstairs. They had waited so long to whip the MacFaddens in the Spelling Bee that staying home instead of celebrating was a total letdown.

"First one to the kitchen gets takeout of their choice!" Salem took off like a shot. "I love sushi!"

Zelda called back to Hilda as she hurried after

him. "If the phone rings, I'll get it. I'm expecting a call from Dr. Wadsworth, the university administrator, about my research grant application."

"Fine." Hilda exhaled with disgust and mumbled, "I'll just sit here and gloat by myself. What fun is that?"

The doorbell rang as she turned toward the living room. Her bummed mood dissipated when she opened the door and saw a short, balding man on the porch. "Mr. Hobson! Come in."

"Thank you." The little man gave her a curt nod as he stepped into the foyer.

Hilda had a hard time containing her excitement. Bernard Hobson was the only accredited clock expert within a hundred miles whom her insurance company would accept as an appraiser. To avoid the prohibitive expense of taking out a new policy, she needed the clock shop inventory appraised so she could update and renew the existing policy—which expired in three days. She needed the insurance before she could renew her business license, which she had to have to operate the shop. There was no magical way around the bureaucratic red tape. However, although she had been hounding him for two weeks, Mr. Hobson had insisted he was too busy to take the job.

"Please, tell me you changed your mind." Hilda giggled, then coughed.

Mr. Hobson scowled. "I might."

"Really?" Hilda put her hand over her mouth to

hold back the chuckles that were suddenly bubbling up in her throat.

Mr. Hobson shifted his weight. "I'll do your appraisal, Ms. Spellman—"

Hilda's shoulders shook as muffled snickers escaped. She was thrilled that Mr. Hobson was willing to squeeze her into his schedule, but that wasn't why she was on the verge of another laughing fit. Either Charlene hadn't removed the spell or she was experiencing temporary spell-echo.

"—for double my usual fee."

That's a bargain compared to the cost of a new policy!

Hilda opened her mouth to take his offer and burst out laughing.

Mr. Hobson's eyes widened, then narrowed as he huffed, "Well! A simple no would have been sufficient."

Hilda tried to talk, but all she could do was laugh.

Squaring his shoulders, Mr. Hobson turned to leave. "I've *never* been so insulted!"

"No, wait—" Hilda sputtered, but she was unable to fight off the waves of laughter. *This can't be happening!*

Mr. Hobson slammed the door behind him.

Still laughing, but feeling miserable, Hilda sank to the floor. As soon as the lingering effects of the hex passed, she'd call Mr. Hobson and apologize. She'd grovel at his feet if necessary! If she didn't

21

get the appraisal, she'd have to close the shop. Or spend the profits from the next six months on insurance.

And she didn't want to explain *that* to her reluctant partner, Zelda.

I think I'll just go laugh myself to sleep, Hilda thought as she crawled to the stairs.

"I'm not calling in a sushi order, Salem." Zelda placed a can of tuna on the counter. "And that's final."

"But Hai Takeout delivers!" Salem pleaded. He was desperate now. *Why does a craving always get worse when you know you can't have what you're craving?*

"No!" Zelda slipped the can into the can opener.

Salem waited until the whirring stopped and sighed. "Then I guess I'll have to settle for tuna."

"You love tuna." Zelda tossed the tin top and reached for a fork.

"Except when my taste buds are primed for sushi. I mean, it's not my fault Sabrina didn't want to go out." Salem rubbed up against Zelda's arm, which had a fifty-fifty chance of wearing down her resolve. "They take credit cards."

"Tuna." Zelda dumped half the flaked fish into his bowl, then set the can aside to answer the phone. "Spellman residence."

Salem took a tiny bite. He adored tuna, but he was still holding out hope that Zelda would relent on the sushi issue. She'd never give in if he looked like he was enjoying it. He grumbled as he chewed for good measure.

"Dr. Wadsworth?" Zelda blinked. "Do I know you?"

"Huh?" Salem swallowed and looked up. Zelda had that look again. *Totally spaced.* That was odd. Florence had removed the memory loss spell.

"What university?" Zelda shrugged. "What's a research grant?" She held the receiver away from her ear and waved at it. "Bye!"

Or not, Salem realized as Zelda turned to him with an inane grin. She had just blown off the university administrator about her grant! Florence's spell was still in effect, which had certain advantages for a cat with a longing for raw fish. If Zelda didn't remember who Dr. Wadsworth was or who he was or who *she* was—maybe she wouldn't remember Hai Takeout, either! He pushed the dish of tuna behind the can opener with his back paw.

"Hi, kitty!" Zelda patted Salem on the head.

Salem moaned and flopped onto his side.

"What's wrong?" Zelda asked.

"Sushi withdrawal," Salem whimpered. "It'll pass—as soon as I eat a Deluxe Sushi Sampler from Hai Takeout. The number's on the refrigerator."

Zelda found the magnetic business card but didn't move toward the phone. She just stood in front of the refrigerator staring at it.

"You have to punch in the numbers," Salem instructed. "On the phone."

"Oh." Nodding, Zelda entered the phone number with painstaking slowness, then held the phone out to the cat.

"Why not? They can't see me!" Salem ordered the sampler, then patiently guided Zelda through the process of finding her credit card in her purse. After the transaction was complete, he sat back with a satisfied sigh.

Zelda hung up the phone, then vacantly glanced at the cat.

"You can go now," Salem said. If the spell was working as it had in the Other Realm, Zelda wouldn't remember ordering the sushi when her brain started working again.

"Okay." Zelda put the credit card on the counter at Salem's feet and paused again. "Go where?"

"How about upstairs for a nice nap?" Salem set his paw on the credit card. *So you won't be around when Hai Takeout delivers.*

"Okay." Still smiling as though she didn't have a care in the world, Zelda sauntered through the kitchen door toward the living room.

Salem chuckled. *What a coup!* His sushi order was on the way and Zelda had given him her credit card! She wouldn't remember that when she recovered her senses, either! But he had to make the most of this extraordinary opportunity before Hilda or Sabrina figured out that Zelda was still under Florence's spell and fixed it. He had always wanted to try ferreting out a few bargains on the Internet auction sites.

"And here's my ticket to buy!" Salem picked up the credit card in his teeth and jumped onto the kitchen table. He flipped open Zelda's laptop computer and logged on to register at Bid-and-Buy.

Chapter 3

Sabrina woke up the next morning feeling more optimistic. Since she hadn't gone out last night, she had gotten ahead on her homework and caught up on her sleep. And nothing terrible had happened because she had a reality check.

Although sitting in my room alone probably wasn't a fair test. Cautiously, she entered the kitchen. Her aunts weren't there, but Salem was sitting on the kitchen table punching the laptop keyboard with the tip of his paw. "Answering e-mail or chatting?"

The cat's head jerked up. He yanked his paw back and slammed the laptop closed. "Uh—yeah! One of the many advantages of the Internet is that everyone makes typos and no one knows I'm a cat."

"Right." Sabrina sat down and pointed a glass of

orange juice and a jelly doughnut. "Aunt Hilda and Aunt Zelda must be sleeping in this morning."

Salem nodded. "Apparently, the Spelling Bee wore them out, too."

"Well, they did wait a long time to get even with the MacFaddens." Sabrina hesitated. Since Salem had been a warlock before being turned into a cat, he might be able to answer the questions she wanted to ask her aunts. "Speaking of the Spelling Bee, what's the real deal on this reality check?"

"I'm not sure I understand the question." Salem leaped to the counter and flipped open a cardboard take-out box.

"I mean, I think it's pretty low to give a first prize that's really a booby prize. Especially for something like the Spelling Bee."

"I still don't understand the question." Salem pulled a seaweed-wrapped fish ball from the box with his teeth and jumped back to the table.

"It makes trouble, right?" Sabrina asked.

"Don't you manage to get into enough trouble on your own?" Salem sniffed the smelly sushi and sighed. "Heavenly."

"Exactly! I don't need a reality check to help." Sabrina sipped her OJ.

Salem paused, then looked up with sudden understanding. "Is that why you were acting so weird last night? Because you think the reality check *makes* trouble?"

"Right. Like turning you into a ghost trapped between realities so you *have* to cash it." Sabrina folded her arms and leaned forward. "I mean, there's got to be a reason *why* the Witches' Council doesn't issue very many of them."

"There is." Salem stretched his neck so his nose was almost touching Sabrina. "If everybody could use reality checks to correct their mistakes, nobody would ever be able to untangle the adjusted time-lines. In addition to the moral considerations, of course."

"What moral considerations?"

"If you *knew* you had a quick fix for every problem or wrong decision, you wouldn't worry about whether you were doing the right thing or not, would you?" Salem's tone was uncharacteristically solemn.

"Probably not." Sabrina squinted thoughtfully and nibbled her doughnut.

"Right. Which is why the Witches' Council has complete control of reality checks and rarely makes one available."

Sabrina brightened. "You mean it works? I can change any event I want without worrying about anything bad happening because of it?"

"Yep."

"And the check can't create some terrible problem that would force me to cash it?" Sabrina's spirits took a definitive upward turn.

"Nope."

"Cool!" Sabrina grinned.

"Totally. Now, if you'll excuse me, I have some unfinished sushi to attend to." Salem tore off a piece of seaweed wrapping, spit it out, and attacked the fish.

Sabrina gulped her juice and grabbed her doughnut. Suddenly, she couldn't wait to get to school. No matter what happened today, she didn't have to worry.

The halls of Westbridge High were frantic with the usual before-first-class activity. Knots of teens gathered in front of lockers to gossip, primp, or search for misplaced homework. Others hung out in front of classroom doors, totally rejecting the idea of taking their designated seats less than fifteen seconds before the bell. Everyone was complaining about the heat.

Everyone except me, Sabrina thought as she moved toward the library. Brad's witch-hunting gene was dormant when it was hot. Harvey's best friend didn't know why he reacted to the presence of magic, but he could sense it. Anyone Brad identified as a witch would be turned into a mouse for a hundred years.

Which was exactly the kind of emergency Aunt Zelda had in mind when she had suggested that Sabrina bank the reality check.

Anxious to return her overdue library books, Sabrina struggled through the student gridlock. The school librarian was almost as bad as Mr. Kraft when it came to strict adherence to rules. With luck, she could just deposit the delinquent volumes in the return book bin and escape before Mrs. Cragmore noticed her.

A lengthy lecture will totally take the edge off this great mood, Sabrina thought as she skirted a traffic snarl at the drinking fountain. Knowing the reality check wasn't a disaster lying in wait had given her a whole new outlook. Her life was usually riddled with one problem or another, whether related to being a teen, a witch, or both. But today she *knew* that no matter what awful problem confronted her, she could solve it with one quick stroke of a pen.

Energized, Sabrina bounced around a corner and found herself face-to-face with a lengthy lecture. "Mr. Kraft!"

"You're smiling." The principal clasped a clip-board to his chest and glowered at her. "Why?"

"Would you believe because I can avert any potential catastrophe by signing my name?" Sabrina winced. She really didn't want to waste her reality check on something minor like getting out of detention, but she couldn't seem to control her flippant tongue around Aunt Zelda's cranky boyfriend.

"Really?" Mr. Kraft handed her a pen and held out the clipboard. "Then sign this."

Trap alert! Sabrina frowned, suspicious. "What is it?"

"Notification that the school board is coming to inspect the school tomorrow. If they don't find everything in perfect order, I could lose my job." Mr. Kraft nervously adjusted his glasses and snatched back his pen. "And why am I telling you?"

"I don't know." Sabrina kept smiling. *But that's one reality I wouldn't want to change!*

"The next person I see kicking a wall will be suspended—indefinitely." Mr. Kraft leaned over to rub a black scuff mark on the wall.

Sabrina savored the prospect of Westbridge High without Mr. Kraft, then realized that Aunt Zelda wouldn't be thrilled if her darling Willard lost his job. She inhaled sharply as her thoughts pursued the logical consequences of that scenario. *What if Aunt Zelda feels so sorry for Mr. Kraft, she agrees to marry him so he won't be homeless and destitute?* Under those circumstances, she would cash her reality check without hesitation.

But since it hasn't happened yet, I'm not gonna worry about it.

"Relax, Mr. Kraft," Sabrina said. "I'm sure the inspection will go well."

"So says the harbinger of more disasters than I can count," Mr. Kraft mumbled, still rubbing the wall.

"Excuse me," a girl's tentative voice said. "Mr. Kraft?"

"Dreama!" Sabrina started when her woefully inadequate witch project from the Other Realm sauntered up. Sabrina had been assigned to help the girl learn how to use magic in the mortal world, which was proving to be a monumental challenge. Dreama's spells almost never worked the way they were supposed to, and when they did, they only lasted ten seconds. Her magic *always* required a reality adjustment.

Sabrina glanced at Mr. Kraft, whose dark demeanor, when he looked up, was as unchanged as the black mark on the wall.

"What is it?" Mr. Kraft snapped.

"We were just leaving." Sabrina took the girl's arm to drag her away, then noticed that Dreama's brow was covered with beads of sweat and her long, thick eyelashes were limp. "Are you sick?"

"No, I'm just wilting in this heat." Dreama cocked an eyebrow at the principal. "Is the air-conditioning broken?"

"No, the air-conditioning isn't broken," Mr. Kraft repeated in a singsong voice. "It's turned off so the school board inspection committee can't accuse me of frivolously spending the taxpayers' money. Deal with it."

"But—" Dreama sagged as Mr. Kraft stalked off. "Now I'm in trouble."

"So am I if I don't get these library books back." Sabrina urged Dreama to walk with her. "Okay, so it's a little hot. Why is that a problem?"

"I can't concentrate when I'm hot," Dreama complained. "And if it's *too* hot, I get dizzy and delirious."

"Define delirious."

"Well, I might think I'm back in the Other Realm and I might—" Dreama sheepishly tugged her ear.

"You might use magic when you can't concentrate and you don't have a clue where you are?" Sabrina gasped. "Or who you're with?"

"I might." Dreama shrugged.

Not what I wanted to hear. Sabrina's thoughts raced as she hurried down the hall. The amount of havoc a delirious Dreama could conjure up was too catastrophic to even think about. Her spells didn't work when she *was* in her right mind! Even though Brad's witch-hunting gene didn't function in the heat, Dreama might still be turned into a mouse if he saw her cast a spell.

Sabrina couldn't take the chance. *If anything bad happens to Dreama, I'll lose my witch license and be deported!*

"Maybe you should go home," Sabrina suggested. "Just until the school inspection is over tomorrow and Mr. Kraft turns the air on again."

"Can't." Dreama shook her head. "I have to learn to deal with *every* problem that comes up here in the mortal world. No exceptions, no excuses."

"Right." Sabrina paused outside the library. Mrs. Cragmore wasn't behind the book checkout counter. At least *that* potential but insignificant problem was working out in her favor. "Okay, don't panic."

"Why not?" Dreama asked, looking slightly frantic.

"Uh—" Sabrina didn't want to come right out

and offer to use the reality check in the event Dreama's bad magic got them both into more hot water than they could stand. However, Dreama's reaction to heat was a problem. Adding panic into the no concentration–delirium mix would practically guarantee a category five fiasco. "There's a solution to every problem, Dreama. You just have to stay cool."

"Literally," Dreama sighed.

"Right!" Sabrina touched her temple. "Just use your head—not your finger—and find a mortal solution. Like, uh—ice packs!"

"Ice packs." Dreama nodded as she walked away. "That might work."

"And that's another crisis averted. I hope." Sabrina dashed into the library. Mrs. Cragmore came out of her office just as Sabrina was putting her overdue books in the return bin. After five minutes of futile, lame excuses, Sabrina left with her library privileges revoked for two weeks. *Inconvenient, but not a major disaster.*

Harvey caught up with her outside her first-period class. "Hey, Sabrina. How's things?"

"Just fine, thanks to the Internet." Sabrina started to explain that she had been barred from the library and still needed to research a science term paper, but Harvey wasn't paying any attention. "Is something wrong?"

"Well, no. Not exactly." Harvey sighed. "My uncle wants to give me a free car."

"Hey, great!" Sabrina was really tired of having to use Brad as a chauffeur every time they wanted to go someplace that required wheels. "What kind?"

"A twenty-year-old Dodge Colt. And it would be great if I could drive it." Harvey sighed and shuffled toward his seat. "It's a wreck."

"But you love fixing up old wrecks and making them go!"

"Yeah, but it's *really* a wreck." Harvey slid behind his desk and sighed. "Paying for parts and insurance will totally wipe out my savings."

"Okay, but since you've been saving for a car, what's the problem?" Sabrina frowned, confused. She was also determined to secure the freedom of motorized mobility for her and Harvey.

"Well, I've got about five hundred dollars, but what if it costs more than that to get the old junker running? Then I won't be able to register it or insure it and I *still* won't be able to drive it." Harvey threw up his hands. "And that's assuming it can be fixed."

"I'll chip in," Sabrina quickly offered. If the old junker turned out to be a money-guzzling lemon, she could always cash in her reality check so Harvey didn't take the car to begin with.

"Thanks!" Harvey's grin flashed on and off again. "But there's something else. I don't have anywhere to put it to work on it. It's such an eyesore, my Dad won't let me park it in the driveway."

"That bad, huh?" Sabrina forced a smile, then focused on the most important factor—being able to drive where they wanted, when they wanted, without an aunt, a parent, or Harvey's best friend the witch-hunter. "Won't Mr. Anderson let you make it a shop project?"

"Now why didn't I think of that?" Harvey slapped his forehead. "Then I'll have help *and* extra credit."

"And a car." Sabrina sighed wistfully. It was amazing how simple the decision-making process was when one had a reality check to fall back on.

Except for one little detail I didn't consider, Sabrina thought, frowning. School had just started and she had already considered using the check to prevent Mr. Kraft from losing his job, to save Dreama from Brad, and to stop Harvey from pouring his life savings into a hopeless car.

But I only have one *reality check!*

☆

Chapter 4

☆

"You did what?" Zelda dropped her coffee cup. A quick point saved it from smashing on the floor.

Hilda winced. "I insulted Mr. Hobson."

"When? Where?" Zelda sank into a chair.

"Last night. Here."

"Here? I don't remember seeing Mr. Hobson." Perplexed, Zelda sat back.

"You were feeding Salem. He came to tell us he'd do the clock shop inventory in the next two days." Hilda absently spooned sugar into her coffee, then dropped her chin in her hand while the spoon stirred. "Although he wanted twice his normal fee to squeeze us into his schedule."

"And you laughed in his face?" Stunned, Zelda stared at Hilda. She kept the accounts for Hickory Dickery Clock, and they were only one acceptable appraisal away from financial ruin. Mr. Hobson's double fee was nothing compared to the cost of a new insurance policy.

"It wasn't my fault!" Hilda said hotly.

"Who's Mr. Hobson?" Salem was sprawled across the closed laptop computer.

"The only clock expert our insurance company trusts," Hilda sighed, then looked at the cat askance. "Isn't that uncomfortable?"

"Actually, no." Salem drew in his legs to curl up on the laptop. "It's uh—warm."

"How could it *not* be your fault?" Zelda's temper flared. Her sister had bought the shop on an impulse. Zelda had agreed to become a partner to make sure the retail venture wasn't a total failure. The store was barely breaking even, but it had potential. However, they couldn't afford to take out a new insurance policy without dipping into their savings or investments, which they had agreed not to do. The shop either made it on its own or it didn't.

"Because it's Charlene MacFadden's fault." Hilda frowned, whipped the spoon out of her cup, and took a long swallow. "Her laughing spell had an echo effect and it hit while I was talking to him."

"An echo?" Zelda's eyes widened. "Are you sure?"

"What else could it be?" Hilda glanced at the clock. "It's been twelve hours since Mr. Hobson was here and I haven't even *felt* like laughing."

Zelda nodded and sighed. The residual echo effects of a spell that wasn't properly cancelled were temporary and faded after a few hours. Charlene had probably created the echo out of spite to get back at Hilda for Sabrina's victory over Agatha. However, the damage was done, and all they could do was try to fix it.

"We've got to get in touch with Mr. Hobson and explain." With a quick point, Zelda changed her rumpled pajamas into dark pants and an elegant, long-sleeved, beige blouse. Flattened blonde hair was instantly curled and combed. "Right away!"

"Agreed." Hilda's fingers snagged in her tangled hair. "I'm going to need more than a quick point to fix this mess. Not to mention a major attitude overhaul if I'm going to eat humble pie." Downing the rest of her coffee, she scurried out the door. "I'll be back in five minutes."

Hoping a moment of deep meditation would relax her, Zelda closed her eyes. She opened them again when she felt Salem's stare boring into her. "What is it, Salem? I can't concentrate when you're staring at me."

"Just wondered how you were feeling this morning." The cat sat up on the laptop and cocked his head.

"I was fine until I found out Hilda may have giggled us right out of business." Draining her cup, Zelda stood up to point the dirty dishes into the sink. Unnerved, she missed, and the china smashed against the cabinet. "Oh, darn!"

"Looks like you need a trip to the finger salon for a recalibration," Salem said.

"No time. Besides, I was getting tired of that pattern anyway." Annoyed, Zelda flipped open the kitchen trash can to dump the shattered pieces. "What's this?"

"Uh—" Salem blinked when Zelda held up an empty Hai Takeout box. "The box from my sushi order."

"What sushi order?" Zelda turned to glower. "I distinctly remember telling you no sushi."

"You changed your mind." Salem held up a paw. "Cat's honor."

Zelda waited for an Honor Patrol cop to pop in and give Salem a citation for lying. When no one burst into the kitchen, she frowned. "I guess I did, but why don't I remember that?"

"Spelling Bee fatigue?" Salem suggested.

"Must be." Shaking her head, Zelda trashed the broken cups and saucers and headed for the foyer to wait for Hilda. Apparently, the tension of watching Sabrina in the Spelling Bee had been more exhausting than she realized. She didn't remember going to bed, either.

As soon as Zelda and Hilda popped out to the clock shop, Salem flipped open the laptop. He had been up half the night entering bids on various objects that had captured his fancy, and he couldn't wait to see what was happening.

"Especially now that I know Zelda doesn't remember anything," Salem sighed with relief. All his bases were covered. Although Zelda hadn't been in her right mind at the time, she *had* ordered the sushi and given him her credit card. He didn't have to be evasive or lie about it. And since her memory lapse was obviously a temporary spell echo like Hilda's laughing fit and not a recurring condition, he didn't have to tell her about *that,* either.

"Besides, if all goes according to plan, I'll make some great deals for practically nothing and she'll thank me!"

Salem logged on to his new Internet account and used a pencil to enter his user ID, SmartCat. He chuckled as he logged on to Bid-and-Buy and held his breath. The first item he had bid on was a Fancy French Gourmet Feast for Four. His mouth watered at the thought of having an "eight-course meal prepared in your own home by a renowned Paris chef." At three o'clock that morning, he had upped the previous bid of thirty-five dollars to forty.

"Let's see where we're at," Salem muttered as he initiated a search. His eyes popped when the bid status window appeared. Somebody called Bargain-Hound had raised the bid to two hundred and fifty dollars!

"A little steep! Even for imported, catered chow." Salem had wanted to surprise Sabrina, Hilda, and Zelda with a scrumptious meal at a bargain price. Disappointed, he moved on to his next selection.

"Nobody else is gonna want a Wacky Wonder Water Zoom."

Salem paused before he hit the search function. He'd have the thirty-foot-high water slide with wading pool installed on the front lawn. If the heat wave continued, he'd make a fortune off the neighborhood kids at a dollar a go. He could even pay Zelda the one hundred and thirty-eight dollars he would have to charge on her credit card to buy it!

With visions of riches swimming in his head, Salem punched up the window and gasped. The bid had risen to fourteen hundred dollars. And Bargain-Hound was the last bidder again!

"Doesn't this guy know the meaning of 'bargain'?" Salem's enthusiasm waned and his frustration mounted as he continued checking his bids. The bids on everything from the Dry Klean Kitty Grooming Mitt to the Tournament Ten Thousand jigsaw puzzle had gone up.

And BargainHound had most of the high bids.

What does some bozo with a dog name want with a cat grooming mitt?

Salem's competitive spirit clicked into gear when he realized he might lose his chance to buy a Kitty Warmer Window Lounge with a Last Forever Battery Pack.

"You're not gonna outbid me on this one, BargainHound." Salem raised the bid from twenty-seven dollars to thirty. Then, utilizing the site's Bid Watch function, Salem listed all his potential purchases in a single display window and settled down to track the action.

Hilda held the phone away from her ear while Mr. Hobson shouted. The shop clocks ticked, whirred, chimed, and bonged around her, adding to the auditory assault, as though they shared the little man's low opinion of her.

Zelda paced, casting an occasional pained glance in Hilda's direction and punching numbers into a calculator. She threw up her hands when a customer banged on the door.

The man pointed to the Closed sign, then to his watch.

Zelda opened the door, whispered something, and the customer left with a smile.

Hilda looked at her curiously and nodded into the phone, waiting for a chance to interrupt the appraiser's tirade. He finally stopped to take a breath, and she plunged in. "Yes, Mr. Hobson, my behavior was inexcusable. I was a rude, ungrateful idiot and I can't even begin to tell you how sorry I am."

"Ms. Spellman"—Mr. Hobson spoke slowly and deliberately—"there is nothing you can do or say that could possibly get me to set foot in your shop—ever!"

"How about the clock of your choice on top of the double fee?" Hilda held up crossed fingers. "We have a wonderful selection of antiques."

Zelda closed her eyes.

"I'll be there in five minutes." Mr. Hobson hung up.

"Yes!" Sagging with relief, Hilda replaced the receiver. "Mr. Hobson is on his way over."

"Excellent!" Zelda pointed the calculator away. "However, I think it would be a good idea to hide the Grandfather Time Clock at the house until he finishes the insurance inventory."

"Right," Hilda agreed. The stately old clock was a priceless Other Realm temporal portal. She and Zelda had been assigned to fix the fates of whatever unfortunate mortal came through it from the past. Changing individual histories had instilled an aspect of chaotic uncertainty in their lives that was sometimes entertaining, occasionally charming, and always fraught with unforeseen hazards. "It's not like we could put in a claim if something happened to it."

"Hardly!" Zelda shuddered. "I'll go point it into the foyer at home."

"What did you tell that guy who was at the door?" Hilda asked.

"To come back in ten minutes for our going-out-of-business sale." Zelda ducked into the back room and shut the door.

"Oh. I think I'll just change that to Closed for Inventory." Hilda zapped up a sign, exchanged it for the regular sign on the door, then set about unlocking display cases. She assumed Zelda was straightening up in the storeroom.

Bernard Hobson arrived in five minutes exactly. He strode in the door like a man with a mission, dropped his suit coat on the counter, and rolled up his sleeves. He checked his watch and made a notation on the clipboard that he pulled out of a briefcase. Then he acknowledged Hilda's presence with a stern scowl. "I'm on the clock as of now."

Trying to maintain a suitably somber expression, Hilda just nodded.

"That was a joke," Mr. Hobson said.

"I'm afraid to laugh," Hilda smiled tightly. "But it was very funny."

"Thank you." He managed a split-second smile before returning to his usual dour demeanor. "I'm just going to take a quick look around to see if you actually *have* a clock I want."

"Of course." Hilda chanced another tight smile as he marched into the storeroom, then felt the rumble of laughter rising in her throat. She clamped her hand over her mouth, and the rumble subsided. She had never heard of a spell echo that lingered indefinitely, although nothing was impossible where magic was concerned. She dashed to the counter to call Salem. He could look up the problem in Sabrina's spell book under anomalies.

The line was busy, but the phone rang the instant she hung up.

"Hickory Dickery Clock!" Hilda laughed. "Dr. Wadsworth! Yes"—giggle, snort—"Zelda's been waiting"—guffaw, guffaw—"to hear from you."

Hilda started laughing and pressed her lips together to muffle the sound while she listened. Dr. Wadsworth was the university administrator who had the final say on whether Zelda received her grant to conduct a scientific study of folk medicine. Although the professor would never know her work was based on magic, Zelda was convinced that certain natural spell ingredients had curative properties that didn't require a magical catalyst.

"You called last night?" Surprised, Hilda covered the mouthpiece and giggled. She thought she had heard the phone ring while she was laughing Mr. Hobson out of the house, but Zelda hadn't said a word. "You must have"—laugh, chortle—"gotten a wrong number."

Dr. Wadsworth informed her that his caller ID box indicated otherwise. He was not amused by Zelda's joke. However, he was willing to give her a chance to explain because of her stellar reputation within the scientific community.

"A meeting in your office at three o'clock today?"—snicker, chortle—"or else?" Knowing that she couldn't contain her runaway hysteria, Hilda quickly ended the conversation. "I'll tell her."

Chuckling, Hilda hung up the phone as Zelda wandered out of the back room. She'd have to leave Zelda to mind the store and handle the cranky appraiser while she popped home to check the spell book. The cure for sustained spell echo was probably simple, like eating lemons to cure hiccups. She couldn't risk infuriating Mr. Hobson with another round of boisterous, inexplicable laughter.

However, before Hilda could draw Zelda aside to deliver Dr. Wadsworth's message and explain that she had to beat a hasty retreat, the appraiser charged out of the back room grinning from ear to ear.

"You did say *any* clock in the shop, didn't you, Ms. Spellman?" Mr. Hobson's steely gray eyes glittered with greed.

"Yes, I'"—Hilda giggled and cleared her throat—"did."

"Then I'll take that one." The little man sighed, clasped his hands, and gazed through the storeroom door.

Hilda laughed, muffled it. "What one?"

"That one!" Mr. Hobson dashed back into the storeroom and threw his arms around the Grandfather Time Clock.

Hilda gasped between giggles and whirled on Zelda. "What were you doing back there? You were supposed to get rid of the Time Clock."

Zelda turned and blinked. "What Time Clock?"

Hilda almost choked. Florence's memory loss spell was still working on Zelda, too! But now she realized the repeating effect wasn't due to a temporary echo effect.

Florence and Charlene zapped us with twenty-four-hour time-release spells!

Chapter 5

Sabrina was still on edge before lunch. Four class periods had passed without any extraordinary incidents. She was finally convinced the reality check was harmless, but she could only use it to change one event. Three potential disasters were brewing.

Candy wrappers and an empty soda can fell out of Sabrina's locker when she opened it to dump her books. She thought about throwing away some of the accumulated trash and decided to do it later. However, after checking to make sure the coast was clear, she cooled off with a blast of arctic air, then hurried toward the cafeteria. Her good mood took a mild dip when Mr. Kraft's voice boomed out of his office.

"You have two choices. Work or detention!"

Since when is hoarding litter in your locker a de-

tention offense? Sabrina stopped dead as the principal marched into the corridor followed by a troop of students armed with buckets, scrub brushes, mops, and brooms.

"Here's the deal." Mr. Kraft clasped his hands in front of him and frowned at his conscripted junior janitors. "If it's dirty, clean it. If everything's clean by the last bell, you're out of here."

The teens scattered to comply.

Mr. Kraft made a notation on his clipboard and noticed Sabrina as he started back into his office. "Are you waiting to volunteer?"

"No! Just glad to see you've got everything under control. Gotta go!" Sabrina walked away, being extra careful not to exceed the hall speed limit. She really wanted Mr. Kraft to pass the school board's inspection tomorrow, but not enough to contribute any muscle to the effort.

Harvey was waiting outside the cafeteria, fanning himself with a spiral notebook. "Hey, Sabrina. What's your secret?"

"Secret? Uh—don't have any!" *Except that I'm a duly licensed witch with all the powers of same,* Sabrina thought. She smiled even though her heart flip-flopped. "Why?"

"You're not sweating." Harvey pulled his damp T-shirt away from his chest.

That's because my arctic chiller hasn't worn off yet.

"Just naturally cool, I guess. Let's eat." Sabrina

bolted past him and raced through the line. After standing in front of the pizza warmer for sixty seconds, her face had a fine sheen of perspiration.

"I've decided to take your advice and take my uncle's old car," Harvey said when they sat down.

"Are you sure that's what you want to do?" Sabrina didn't want to discourage him, but the old Dodge didn't come with a guarantee. "What if it can't be fixed? Or you can't afford insurance and plates when you get it running?"

"Not a problem." Harvey grinned. "Mr. Anderson gave me permission to make it a shop project so I don't have to worry about where to put it."

"And you'll get credit for the work!" Sabrina brightened.

"Better. I'll get a discount at the parts store for anything I can't find at the junkyard because it's a school project. I'm pretty sure my budget can handle that and the registration and insurance."

"Wow!" Sabrina grinned. "That's—amazing!"

Harvey leaned forward. "Taking it to the school shop was a great idea, Sabrina. Thanks."

"Glad to help." A wave of relief washed over Sabrina. She could stop worrying about Harvey's new old car project.

"I can't wait to get started." Harvey wiped sweat off his forehead with his napkin. "Brad and I are gonna use his car to tow it into the shop tomorrow morning."

"Oh. That's, uh—nice." Sabrina took a bite of

pizza to keep from voicing her opinions about Brad. Brad didn't know he had the witch-hunting gene or why he was uncomfortable when she was around. She knew why he made *her* uncomfortable, but that didn't diminish the inherent danger. The less time she spent with Brad the better, but he was hard to avoid since he was Harvey's best friend.

"Now there's another cool idea," Harvey said.

Sabrina followed his gaze toward the cafeteria door.

Dreama strode in carrying a clipboard. She had plastic bags filled with melting ice taped to her wrists and ankles, tied to her belt, and draped around her neck. She left a trail of dripping water as she came over to the table.

She looks ridiculous, Sabrina thought, *but at least she isn't delirious and making magical mayhem.*

"Ice packs." Harvey nodded, impressed. "Are they working? Keeping you cool, I mean."

"Apparently." Dreama smiled. "I haven't had a dizzy spell or grown a glacier in the halls."

Harvey laughed and blotted his neck with Sabrina's napkin. "An ice age sounds pretty good right now."

"She has such a weird sense of humor, doesn't she?" Sabrina shot Dreama a warning glance, which the girl totally missed or ignored.

"Well, since I can't whip up an iceberg, we have to force Mr. Kraft to turn the air-conditioning back on." Dreama's brow knit with stubborn intent.

"Forget it, Dreama." Harvey raised a skeptical eyebrow. "Nobody can force Mr. Kraft to do anything."

"Right." Sabrina eyed Dreama pointedly. "You haven't *done* anything yet, have you?"

"Oh, don't worry. I've got a totally mortal plan." Dreama handed Sabrina the clipboard. "And over a hundred signatures on my petition so far."

"You're circulating a petition to get the air turned back on?" Sabrina took the clipboard and nodded her approval. Dreama was using her head, which was good. However, the petition was useless. Mr. Kraft ran the school like a police state, and a piece of paper wouldn't counter his no-air edict, no matter how many signatures Dreama collected. But Dreama was trying so hard to follow the mortal rules that Sabrina didn't have the heart to dampen her spirits with the blunt truth. She signed.

"I'll sign." Harvey patted his pockets. "Got a pen?"

"Sign what?" Brad slid into the seat beside Harvey and gave Dreama a disbelieving once-over. "Your water bags are leaking."

"They're ice packs and they wouldn't be leaking if it wasn't so hot in here." Dreama took her pen and clipboard back from Harvey after he signed, and she handed them to Brad. "Want to sign my petition?"

"What petition?" Mr. Kraft asked.

Sabrina jumped, spilling her milk when the principal appeared behind Dreama.

"And why are you dripping all over the floor?" Mr. Kraft scowled at Dreama.

Dreama swallowed hard but stood her ground. "A petition to have the air-conditioning turned back on. It's too hot in here."

Mr. Kraft's eyes narrowed as he snatched Dreama's clipboard away from Brad.

Brad held up his hands. "I didn't sign it!"

"Lucky you. I want to see who did." Mr. Kraft's mouth twitched with a slight smile as he scanned the signatures on the list. His grin widened when he looked back at Dreama. "Excellent work."

What? Sabrina frowned.

Dreama beamed. "Does that mean you'll turn the air back on?"

"No, it means you've got detention for inciting student unrest and leaving a trail of puddles." Mr. Kraft ripped the petition off the clipboard and handed the clipboard back to the shocked girl. "Or you can report to the kitchen for clean-up duty immediately."

"You can't give her detention for exercising her rights of free speech!" Sabrina rushed to Dreama's defense. "A petition is a totally peaceful protest against cruel and unusual climate control. It's not like Dreama started a riot."

"It's so hot nobody has the energy to riot," Harvey muttered.

"Ms. Spellman." Mr. Kraft sighed wearily and adjusted his glasses. "I have *total* control of everything in this school. Nobody circulates a petition on my watch—especially during a school board inspection."

"But that's un-American!" Sabrina huffed.

"Take it up with your congressperson," Mr. Kraft sighed with satisfaction. "In the meantime, since you contributed to this outrageous attempt to usurp my authority with your signature, you'll report for immediate KP, too. Scrubbing pots and pans with your rebel friend."

"But—" Sabrina's protest died in her throat.

"Mr. Kinkle," Mr. Kraft continued, "I believe the trophies in the display cabinet could use a polish. Maybe Mr. Alasaro would like to help."

"I didn't sign it!" Brad's eyes flashed.

"Yes, quite." Still smiling, Mr. Kraft held up Dreama's petition. "But all *these* people did. So if you'll excuse me, I'm off to hunt them down."

"So much for that idea!" Dreama threw up her hands as the principal walked away.

"You'll get another one, Dreama," Sabrina assured her. "As soon as you cool off."

"Which won't be easy without air-conditioning," Harvey said.

Sabrina thought about cashing in the reality check to save the entire student body from further harassment by Mr. Kraft, but rejected it. The situation was annoying, but it didn't qualify as a disaster of cataclysmic proportions. As long as it was hot, Brad wasn't subconsciously tuned into magic.

And although it wasn't fair for Mr. Kraft to enlist student labor on trumped-up charges, nobody would have to stay after school. A few would probably be glad to miss afternoon classes. She'd definitely be better off if Westbridge High passed the school board inspection and Mr. Kraft kept his job. Besides, she could make the whole kitchen sparkle with a single point when no one was looking.

And I can keep Dreama on ice and delirium-free in the walk-in cooler!

Maybe multiple disasters weren't looming on the horizon after all.

Salem stared at the Bid Watch window with intense feline patience. Without twitching or blinking, he waited for BargainHound to make the next move.

Like a lion stalking prey, Salem thought with resolve. *And it's almost time to go in for the kill.*

The bids on his target items had risen slowly all morning, inching up by one-, five-, and ten-dollar increments. Most of the other bidders had dropped out when the rivalry between SmartCat and BargainHound had become apparent, and the bidding pace had picked up. The dog guy was a worthy opponent who knew how to bait and tease, which had made the game interesting—for a while.

Now Salem intended to start bagging his prizes

with a stunning strategy. He wasn't going to waste any more time on pathetic five- and ten-dollar raises. BargainHound would flinch and forfeit when he—or she—realized the *cat* meant business.

Salem tensed when BargainHound raised the bid on the Screaming Banshee Alarm Clock from Salem's last offer of one hundred forty-three dollars to one hundred forty-seven dollars. The cat laughed and unsheathed his claws.

"That clock is a must have," the cat muttered. Hilda and Zelda could use the limited edition hand-crafted timepiece for security in the clock shop. The wooden frame was delicately carved in a traditional Celtic pattern, one of Hilda's favorite designs. In addition to keeping precision time, the clock could also be installed and armed to sound a bloodcurdling shriek if someone tried to break into the store after hours.

"Cheap Pooch will never know what hit him!" Salem picked up his pencil and raised his bid by a hundred dollars. "So how do you like *that*, Bargain-Hound?"

Not much, Salem realized when BargainHound immediately raised the bid on the Wacky Wonder Water Zoom to three thousand five hundred and fifty.

Salem paused to calculate how many slide rides he could squeeze into an hour multiplied by how many hours it would take to pay off the first attraction in the Spellman Front Yard Amusement Park.

Provided the neighborhood kids didn't run out of money first. "No problem! I'll just advertise on the web!"

Salem raised the bid on the water slide another two hundred dollars.

BargainHound upped the price on the Water Zoom two hundred more, then jumped to the pocket-sized combination color TV, cell phone, and calculator.

"Five hundred and sixty-four!" Salem fumed. He had no idea how much credit was available on Zelda's card, but he knew it wasn't enough to win the bidding war. BargainHound was determined to beat him no matter what it cost.

Salem sat up, blinked, and smiled. His new strategy would still work. He might not get the goodies, but he *could* make sure BargainHound went bankrupt outbidding him.

With gritted teeth, Salem plunged into the battle of the bids with a vengeance.

Zelda pulled back when she and Hilda reached Dr. Wadsworth's outer office door at the university. "This is a really bad idea, Hilda."

"It wasn't my idea," Hilda reminded her.

"I know," Zelda sighed. She had been spaced out in the back room of the clock shop with Mr. Hobson when the university administrator had called. "But couldn't you have made an appointment for tomorrow *after* the twenty-four-hour time-release spells wear off?"

"Yes," Hilda nodded, "except I didn't know we were under time-release spells at the time. Besides, Dr. Wadsworth wasn't open to negotiation. He was quite loud and *very* clear. Today at three or forget your grant."

Zelda sighed again. The time-release sequence incorporated into the MacFadden sisters' spells was erratic. Hilda could become a laughing maniac and she could forget everything she ever knew at any time—without warning. The spells would automatically end that evening, but that might be too late to save her grant or the Grandfather Time Clock.

Hilda glanced at her watch. "It's two minutes to three."

"Come on, then." Zelda reached for the doorknob. "And remember. If I suddenly go brainless, get me out of there immediately."

"Right. That's why I agreed to come with you." Hilda frowned, worried. "Have you thought of an explanation for giving Dr. Wadsworth the brush-off yet?"

"No, I'm hoping for some on-site inspiration." Zelda braced herself and walked into the reception room.

The austere decor reflected the strict administrator's personality. Straight-backed wooden chairs lined one wall. Somber portraits of persons unknown hung on the walls. There were no magazines, books, or ornaments on the tables.

The thin, stern woman who worked as Dr.

Wadsworth's secretary sat behind an uncluttered desk in the reception room. A plaque engraved with her name identified her as Miss Jorkel. Her demeanor and bearing were as starched as her high buttoned collar. Her thin mouth puckered with disapproval as she peered at Zelda and Hilda. "Ms. Spellman, I presume."

"Yes." Hilda and Zelda answered in unison.

"I have a three o'clock appointment with Dr. Wadsworth," Zelda replied as she stared back. Her finger twitched, but she controlled an impulse to change the annoying woman into a worm.

"Yes, of course." The secretary picked up the phone and punched a button. "Ms. Spellman to see you, sir." She wrinkled her nose as she pointed toward the administrator's office door. "You can go right in."

Hilda paused to sneer back. "Did you sleep through your sensitivity training or skip it altogether?"

Zelda yanked Hilda into Dr. Wadsworth's office.

Dr. Wadsworth was scribbling on a file and did not look up when they stopped in front of his desk. Middle-aged, short, and portly, he had a double chin and a full head of white hair that needed a trim.

Hilda stiffened and cleared her throat.

Zelda nudged her and shook her head. Under the circumstances, it was better to overlook the man's rudeness than to forfeit the slim chance she still had to get her grant. She pushed Hilda down into a chair, then seated herself. She set her briefcase on the floor and waited.

Dr. Wadsworth threw down his pen, raised his head, and folded his hands. His gaze shifted from Hilda to Zelda and back again. "Good afternoon, ladies. At least you're on time."

"Time is our business," Hilda said brightly. "We own a clock shop."

"Actually, it's *her* clock shop," Zelda added. Science was her primary occupation, and she didn't want to give the administrator the wrong impression. "I'm a silent partner in the family business— more or less."

"I see. Then you must be Zelda." Dr. Wadsworth gave Zelda a curt nod, then glanced at Hilda. "And you are?"

"Hilda. Zelda's sister."

"And why are you here?" Dr. Wadsworth asked, puzzled.

"Hilda's also my research assistant." Zelda smiled tightly. She didn't want Dr. Wadsworth to think she needed her sister present for moral support, either. "Which is why I asked her to attend this meeting."

"I see." Dr. Wadsworth sat back and tugged on his jacket, which had bunched up around his ample waist. "Before we proceed, I'd appreciate an explanation for our telephone conversation last night."

"I can't wait to hear it," Hilda said softly.

"I am *so* sorry about that, Dr. Wadsworth." Zelda tried to look contrite. "Our neighbor is quite elderly and somewhat forgetful."

"Your elderly neighbor answered your phone?" the administrator asked, incredulous. "Why?"

Hilda jumped in. "She wanders into our kitchen by mistake now and then."

"Right," Zelda nodded. The fabricated story was so bizarre that she was sure Dr. Wadsworth wouldn't suspect they had made it up. "And then she wanders out again. Sometimes we don't even know she was there. Hilda and I were not aware that you had called last night, Dr. Wadsworth."

"Not until you called the clock shop this morning," Hilda clarified.

"I see. How odd." Dr. Wadsworth's left eye twitched slightly, but he seemed satisfied. He took a form from the file and scanned it. "Let's get down to business then, shall we? Before I can give final approval on your research grant, Zelda—"

Where am I?

The man behind the desk looked up. "May I call you Zelda to avoid confusion?"

"Zelda?" She pointed to her chest, hesitated, then nodded. Zelda was a nice name. "Okay."

"Yes, well—" The man coughed. "I have a few questions. How long have you been working with medicinal herbs?"

Zelda twisted in her chair to look around the room. It was dark and drab and full of old books.

She didn't like it. It wasn't pretty like the lady sitting next to her. The lady kicked her in the ankle.

"Ow!"

"Herbs?" The pretty lady smiled, but she wasn't being nice.

Zelda pouted. "You're mean."

The pretty lady's eyes got very big. Her mouth stretched into a funny smile.

"What do I mean?" The man leaned toward Zelda and rephrased the question. "I want to know how long you've been working with natural remedies?"

Zelda shrugged. "I don't know. What are—"

"Resumé!" The pretty lady giggled, then picked up a case and set it on Zelda's lap. Her face got red as she looked inside and pulled out a paper. "This should answer all your"—giggle, smirk—"questions, Dr. Wadsworth."

"I *have* your sister's resumé." The doctor scowled at the pretty lady. "I'd like *Zelda* to answer my questions, if you don't mind."

Zelda smiled at the man. She didn't know any answers, but she liked questions. She had a lot of them. "Do I know you?"

"Excuse me?" The man's eye twitched faster.

The pretty lady started to laugh and pressed her lips together. Her shoulders shook.

The pretty lady and the man were funny, but nothing held Zelda's attention longer than a few seconds.

"What's that?" Zelda pointed to a framed paper on the wall behind the man. It was crooked, and she wanted to straighten it. The framed glass-covered paper whipped one way, then the other, then crashed to the floor.

"What the—" The man jumped out of his chair.

The pretty lady chuckled. She held her stomach with one hand and put the other over her mouth.

Zelda's finger felt tingly. She blew on it, then shook it.

All the papers on the man's desk zipped into the air.

"What's going on here?" The man batted at the papers buzzing his head.

The pretty lady laughed aloud. Water came out of her eyes. "I think we'd better"—chortle, snort— "go."

"Why?" Zelda asked. As the pretty lady grabbed the case and pulled her to her feet, a tall container by the door caught her attention. She wanted to see what was on the other end of the sticks with curved handles inside it, and she pointed. "What's that?"

"An umbrella stand." The pretty lady laughed harder when the long sticks shot toward the ceiling and whooshed open into upside-down parachutes. They began to twirl and drift around the room.

"What's happening?" The man flattened himself against the wall and yelled. "Help! Help!"

The door flew open. A skinny lady stared into the room and screamed.

Startled, Zelda pointed again. The door slammed closed before the loud lady could enter.

The pretty lady grabbed Zelda by the shoulders. She ducked a drifting umbrella and a flock of swooping papers and spoke between laughs and gasps for air. "Do exactly as I say, Zelda. Understand?"

"Okay."

"Repeat after me." Hilda took a deep breath and whispered in Zelda's ear. When she was finished, Zelda recited the silly words.

> *"Umbrella choppers, paper planes,*
> *grounded when I point again."*

"Point!" Hilda ordered.

Zelda pointed, then flinched as open umbrellas crash-landed and papers glided to the office floor. A fuzzy vibration zipped through her head. She blinked, then looked around her, aghast. "What happened, Hilda?"

"Oh, you're back!" Hilda paused to catch her breath, then glanced at the petrified administrator. He was still plastered against the wall, his eyes bulging with fright. "Well, let's just say it's a good thing Sabrina has a reality check."

"If she hasn't cashed it yet!" Zelda bolted for the door.

Chapter 6

Salem woke from his catnap with a start. He had fallen asleep with his chin resting on the laptop keyboard, and his jaw was numb from lack of circulation. He yawned, stretched to relieve the kinks in his legs, and glanced at the monitor screen. The little colored screen-saver fish swimming through a cyber-ocean reminded him that he had slept through lunch.

"Food first. Then I'll watch BargainHound go broke!"

Salem jumped to the floor and hooked a claw under the cabinet door. Hilda and Zelda wouldn't be home from the clock shop until after six, and Sabrina was working at the coffeehouse after school. "Is it my fault nobody's around to open a can? Nooooo."

He pulled a cardboard container of dried clam and oyster treats off the shelf and popped the plastic lid with his teeth. After gobbling three of the tasty morsels, Salem stuffed as many as he could carry into his mouth. He leaped back onto the table, dropped the treats, and went back for more. When he had accumulated a sizeable pile, he flopped back down in front of the laptop screen.

"Those should keep me from starvation's door a while." Salem unsheathed and sheathed his claws a few times to warm up, then moved the track ball to clear the animated fish from the screen. A red-alert light blinked on the Bid Watch window. The bidding was about to close on one of his items.

Salem closed his eyes to savor the moment before checking. BargainHound had countered every single bid SmartCat had made all day. Before he had fallen asleep, Salem had raised all the bids on everything BargainHound was determined to get. The dog guy didn't seem to care that the prices had risen well past the actual value of the products. They were both bidding for the thrill of the contest.

"Boy, will BargainHound be surprised when I give up and stick *him* with all that stuff!" Salem chuckled, sighed, and opened his eyes to study the screen. The blinking red light beside the Tournament Ten Thousand jigsaw puzzle changed to a blinking green Going.

Salem chewed another treat as he read the item info line and almost choked. *"What?"*

His last bid had been two hundred seventy-eight dollars.

The bid was *still* two hundred seventy-eight dollars, and SmartCat was listed as the final bidder.

"Hey, BargainHound! Where are you?"

The blinking green Going changed to a blinking red Going.

Panicking, Salem called up the Internet immediate-message window and typed a note to Bargain-Hound.

Hey, Fido! What happened? Lose the scent or what? I'm gonna get the tournament puzzle! Unless you think you can stop me! SmartCat.

Salem pushed Send and crossed his front paws. He was absolutely positive BargainHound wouldn't be able to resist a challenge from a cat. He certainly hoped so.

The red Going blinked faster.

A minute passed with no response from Bargain-Hound.

Maybe the pup is taking a nap, too!

Stunned, Salem watched helplessly as the blinking red Going became a stable red Gone!

"Oh, no." He winced when the invoice window appeared. With premium overnight shipping and handling charges, he had just bought a ten-thousand-piece jigsaw puzzle that normally sold for thirty-nine ninety-five for over three hundred dollars!

On Zelda's credit card!

Don't panic! Salem paused to collect his thoughts. Zelda probably wouldn't even notice the charge. And even if she did, he could plead ignorance about how the bid site worked. And suggest that they could give the puzzle to Sabrina for Christmas. Or save it to put together as a family some cold winter afternoon when they didn't have anything else to do.

"Things could be a lot worse," Salem muttered as he picked up the pencil to push the Back button. "I could have gotten stuck with the Wacky Wonder Water Zoom for seven grand."

Salem quickly scanned the rest of the information lines in the Bid Watch window. His heart skipped a beat and his breath caught in his throat.

All his last bids were *still* the top bids!

Including the Wacky Wonder Water Zoom for seven thousand four hundred fifty-six dollars!

"Okay." Salem took a deep breath, then shouted, "Panic!"

Sabrina was in high spirits when she arrived at the coffeehouse for her afternoon shift. Dreama had stayed cool, and her magic had stayed under control in the cafeteria's walk-in refrigerator all afternoon. Dreama had popped back to the Other Realm grumbling about Mr. Kraft's unfair labor practices, but at least the school was still standing.

And clean!

Sabrina grinned as she bopped through the coffeehouse door. She had left the cafeteria and kitchen gleaming with a few carefully executed points. The rest of the building looked almost as good because Mr. Kraft had manipulated most of the student body into maid service duty during afternoon classes. If white walls and squeaky-clean floors meant anything to the school board inspection committee, his job was secure.

"I'd rather deal with Mr. Kraft at school than have him lounging in my living room as a permanent guest." Relieved, Sabrina walked behind the counter and dropped her books in a corner. The late lunch crowd was gone and the after-class college crowd hadn't started to arrive, which gave her a few minutes to unwind and shift gears.

"Hey, Sabrina!" Josh came in through the back door. "You're early."

"Yeah, well." Sabrina slipped an apron over her head and shrugged. "Scouring junkyards for 1979 Dodge Colts isn't my idea of a fun way to shop. So here I am!"

"You're in a good mood." Josh shook out a new plastic trash bag and placed it into the counter trash container.

"Couldn't be better." Sabrina dumped old coffee into the sink and rinsed out the pot. It had been a good day. All the potential problems had sorted themselves out just fine. Since she had to work, she didn't even mind that Harvey was spending quality male-bonding time rummaging through rusty, greasy car parts with Brad. "I've got a reality check and I don't even need it!"

Josh laughed. "You've got the most charming sense of humor. Weird, but charming."

"Thanks," Sabrina sighed, content with the world.

For a change, life was just about perfect. She was completely over her crush on the pleasant, handsome, college-aged Josh, which had almost destroyed her relationship with Harvey. She and Harvey had made up after they both realized neither one of them wanted anyone else. Josh didn't have any hard feelings, and they had become good friends. He was also the best boss a teenaged witch could ask for. He hadn't even *thought* about firing her when the partying zombies wrecked the café on Halloween!

Josh wiped down the sandwich board and counter. "What do you know about the stock market?"

"Not much." Sabrina started the coffeemaker. "It goes up. It goes down. That's about it. Why?"

"I just got a hot tip on a new technical stock and I can't decide whether to move on it or not." Josh tossed his rag in the sink and sighed.

"How hot?"

"Scalding." Josh grinned. "The company's called A. I. Technologies. Imagine artificially intelligent *personal* computers. I mean, machines that actually develop personalities! Sort of like an electronic pet that thinks for itself, talks, *and* balances your checkbook."

After living with a flesh and blood talking cat with a mind of his own, Sabrina wasn't sure she'd want to cope with a machine that had its own agenda. But then, Salem couldn't balance a checkbook.

"So what's stopping you?" Sabrina asked, curious. "No money to invest?"

"No, I've got a couple thousand in the bank." Josh stared at the floor, rubbing his chin.

"Then I guess you don't really need the twenty I was going to offer to loan you." Sabrina's definition of high finance was a hundred-dollar balance in her savings account after expenses and a five-dollar tip.

"Uh—that wouldn't even buy one share, but I appreciate the thought."

"Oh." Two thousand dollars sounded like a small fortune to Sabrina. It *was* a small fortune in teen terms.

"I've been saving to get a head start on paying off my student loan after I graduate. I'm not sure I want to risk the money on a hot hunch." Josh sighed. "Although, if my source is right, I could double my investment in a couple days."

"Or lose it all," Sabrina said.

"Or break even," Josh added.

Sabrina nodded, then voiced her thoughts aloud.

"Well, breaking even wouldn't be so bad. You wouldn't lose, and there's a chance you'll be able to sell the stock for more than it cost. Maybe even double your money."

"You're right. I should go for it. Nobody ever gets anywhere without taking a few chances." Josh whipped off his apron and dashed around the counter.

"Wait, I didn't mean—"

Josh paused at the door. "I have to admit the element of risk is rather exciting. I feel energized! Thanks, Sabrina! I'll be back in an hour."

"Wait!" Sabrina started after him, but Josh was already out the door and gone.

"Well, that's just great." Sabrina sank onto the overstuffed couch. "What if he blames *me* when he loses his life savings?"

Since she had pointed out that he had two out of three chances to keep or increase his hard-earned cash, she felt responsible for Josh's decision—at least partially. He was always so understanding and nice that she'd feel awful if the stock price went down instead of up. Her spirits bottomed out for a few seconds, then suddenly bounced back.

"Why am I worried?" Sabrina jumped up and rushed back to the counter when a local poet wandered in and took his usual seat by the window. The problems at school were manageable, and everything was fine at home. "If Josh goes broke, I can fix it with my reality check!"

* * *

Sabrina was still feeling wonderful when she arrived home just before six. Josh had been a blast when he'd returned from buying fifty shares of AITE through an Internet brokerage. He had opened an account months before but had never had the nerve to actually buy. Now that he had completed his first market transaction, he was like a little boy waiting for Santa Claus. He couldn't wait to track his stock on-line tomorrow.

"And he let me leave early. Definitely a plus." Sabrina carried her books through the living room toward the kitchen, the last place she had seen Aunt Zelda's laptop. She still had to finish researching the human habitation of Mars, the subject of her science term paper. Although she had firsthand knowledge of the red planet, she was sure a report on the witches' ski resort and luxury hotel wouldn't be acceptable.

"Hi, Salem."

The cat slammed the laptop closed.

"Does that mean you're done with the computer?" Sabrina dropped her books on the table.

"Why?" Salem's tail swished and his whiskers drooped.

"Because I've got to surf the web for some science info." Sabrina sat down and reached for the laptop.

Salem fell on top of it. "You can't."

"Why not?" Sabrina eyed him narrowly. "Did you hack into my e-mail again?"

"No!" Salem shook his head, then began to bawl. "Worse!"

"Should I take a couple aspirin?" Sabrina's mood took another downswing. The cat was obviously upset and that always meant he had gotten himself into some kind of terrible trouble. "I have a feeling this is going to give me a splitting headache. And I was having such a good day!"

"So was I until"—sniffle, sob—"un-until that rotten d-d-dog"—gasp for air, sniffle—"p-person l-let me h-have everything I wanted! Waa-hah!"

"Stop sobbing, Salem. You're not making any sense." Sabrina pointed up a tissue and held it to the cat's nose. "Blow."

Salem blew, gulped more air, and stifled his pathetic sobs. "You've got to help me."

"Hard to do when I don't know what's wrong." The tissue disappeared into the trash can with a flick of Sabrina's wrist. "So some dog gave you a bunch of gifts?"

"No." Salem sniffled, then sighed. "Bargain-Hound didn't top my bids at Bid-and-Buy on the web and I bought it all! I'm doomed." He went limp.

"So you bought a few things." Sabrina patted his head. "Maybe I can help you out. How much do you need?"

Salem hung his head and muttered.

"How much?"

"Nine thousand seven hundred and ninety-four dollars." The cat cringed.

Sabrina just stared at him a moment. "Who let you run up a huge bill like that?"

"Zelda's credit card has a ten-thousand-dollar limit," Salem explained.

Sabrina leaped to her feet. "You took Aunt Zelda's credit card?"

"No, Zelda gave it to me. She doesn't *remember* giving it to me because Florence's memory-loss spell kicked in again, but she *did* give it to me." Salem stretched toward Sabrina, his eyes wide with desperation. "But don't tell her!"

"She's going to find out you maxed her card when she gets the bill!" Sabrina threw up her arms. If a freethinking, talking cat could put the family into the poorhouse in one day, how much chaos would a freethinking computer with total access to the world wide web create? Maybe Josh hadn't made such a wise investment after all.

"No, she won't," Salem purred. "Not if you use your reality check to take me back to the moment I decided to bankrupt BargainHound."

"Oh." Sabrina sat back down. If she used the check to help Salem, she wouldn't have it to help Josh if he got into trouble. "Does it matter whether I use it to save you from Aunt Zelda's wrath today or tomorrow?"

Salem lapsed into pensive thought. "I suppose not. If Zelda banishes me to the dungeon on a diet of discount kibble and water tonight and you change reality tomorrow, my punishment wouldn't have happened."

"Right. Then if it's all the same to you, I'll wait.

Just in case you win the lottery and can pay off your debt."

Sabrina exhaled wearily. Josh would probably make a killing in the stock market before *that* happened, but she wouldn't know until tomorrow. She should probably be grateful that she only had two potential catastrophes to lose sleep over.

"Sabrina!" Hilda shouted as she popped into the kitchen with Aunt Zelda. They both looked panic-stricken.

Aunt Zelda wrung her hands. "Have you cashed your reality check yet?"

Oh, boy. Sabrina wilted.

Chapter 7

Zelda dragged herself downstairs the next morning. Humiliated by her behavior in Dr. Wadsworth's office, she had gone straight to bed to sleep off the rest of Florence MacFadden's twenty-four-hour time-release spell. Although she didn't have to worry about lapsing into a spaced-out stupor again, her university grant was a no-go and her scientific reputation was ruined.

The university administrator and his secretary were convinced she and Hilda were responsible for their nervous breakdowns. Fortunately, they also thought the flying-umbrella-and-paper attack was a hallucination.

"But Dr. Wadsworth still thinks I'm a brainless bimbo," Zelda mumbled as she shuffled into the kitchen.

Hilda was on the phone. "That soon?"

"Is that the hospital?" Zelda whispered. She had asked the attending physician to call with a report about Dr. Wadsworth's and Miss Jorkel's conditions.

Hilda shook her head. "Yes, well, you're absolutely right, Mr. Hobson. A deal's a deal. We'll see you in an hour."

Zelda sank into a chair opposite Hilda and pointed a steaming cup of double chocolate mocha café. The chocolate probably wouldn't cure her depression, but it would taste good. "I take it Mr. Hobson doesn't want another clock."

"Mr. Hobson won't even consider *six* other clocks." Hilda rolled her eyes and zapped up a plate of Bavarian creme doughnuts. "He expects to finish the appraisal by closing today, and he's already arranged for a truck to pick up the Grandfather Time Clock."

Salem was curled up on the laptop again. Although Zelda wasn't in the mood to check her e-mail or her research notes on medicinal herbs, which were worthless without the university grant, his recent attachment to the portable computer was curious and irritating.

The cat opened one eye. "While you're at it, how about a nice plate of shrimp Rangoon?"

"It's not on your diet." Hilda started to take a huge bite of chocolate-covered pastry, caught the cat staring at her, and flicked her finger. A plate of fried wontons stuffed with shrimp appeared on the table. "One word, Salem, and they're gone."

Salem smiled and stretched to reach the plate. With his back half still draped over the laptop, he dug in.

Zelda ignored the cat's odd territorial claim on the computer. They had more important issues to address at the moment. "We can't let Mr. Hobson take the Grandfather Time Clock, Hilda. Not even if it means closing the clock shop because we can't afford to renew the insurance."

"I know." Hilda polished off the first doughnut and picked up another. "Sabrina's reality check is our only hope."

Zelda nodded.

Salem stopped eating long enough to sigh, catching Hilda's attention. She pulled the plate away. "Sabrina didn't happen to mention what she had decided before she left this morning, did she, Salem?"

"Not a word," Salem said.

Hilda exhaled with exasperation. "You have my permission to talk about anything except my culinary indulgences. What did Sabrina say?"

"She said she'd get back to me." Salem heaved another sigh, then looked up sharply. "You, I meant. She said she'd get back to *you*. I think she's stalling, though."

"Why?" Hilda asked.

"She asked me if it would make any difference

when she cashed the check." Salem snatched another shrimp Rangoon off the plate.

"Actually, it wouldn't matter," Hilda said. "Whatever she decided to change would still be changed—eventually."

"Oh, my." Zelda's hand shook as she set down her cup. "What if Sabrina promised to fix something for someone else?"

"Yeah!" Salem's ears perked up. "What if?"

"That might explain why she ran out of here last night to call Josh yelling 'Sell! Sell!' " Sagging, Hilda pointed the doughnuts away and replaced them with a fizzy antacid. "I'm not going to worry. Sabrina won't let us down."

Zelda sipped her coffee and concentrated on feeling wretched. She and Hilda weren't directly responsible for their problems because they had been under the influence of the MacFaddens' spells. Still, it wasn't fair to ask Sabrina to use her rare reality check to help them.

Hilda drank the antacid and made a face. "Maybe we should have told her that the penalty for giving a unique Other Realm artifact like the Grandfather Time Clock to a mortal is having our powers revoked."

"*And* fifty years of hard labor scrubbing cauldrons in the Little Witch Pre-school Practice Dome," Zelda added.

"With no hope of parole," Hilda groaned.

"Beats being a cat," Salem mumbled.

Brakes squealed outside. A few seconds later the sound of rumbling gears shook the floor.

"What's that?" Zelda asked.

Salem stiffened. "I didn't hear anything."

Someone pounded on the back door.

"Who's that? It's not even eight o'clock yet." Rolling her eyes, Hilda rose to check.

"Nobody!" Salem sprang off the table and tried to block the door.

"What's the matter with you?" Hilda cried as she picked him up and opened the door.

A man in a blue uniform shoved a clipboard at Hilda. "Delivery for Zelda Spellman. Sign here."

Hilda's mouth fell open. She stared out the door, speechless.

"I don't remember ordering anything." Zelda quick-changed to make herself presentable and joined Hilda at the door. A flatbed truck loaded with large cartons and huge, brightly colored cylindrical metal tubes was parked in the driveway. "Do you know anything about this, Salem?"

"It was an accident! I was framed!"

Zelda crossed her arms. "And?"

"And, uh—" Salem swallowed hard. "Well, since you're not going to own a clock shop or be a professional scientist anymore . . . want to help me run the Spellman Wacky Wonder Water Zoom?"

The school was still deserted when Sabrina arrived. She had left the house early so she could see

Harvey's old wreck when he and Brad towed it into the shop—and because she couldn't face her aunts and Salem. Her thoughts were in turmoil as she hustled through the empty hallways toward the auto shop.

Aunt Hilda and Aunt Zelda weren't facing potential disasters. They had collided with catastrophe compliments of the MacFadden sisters' spells. Salem, on the other hand, was just a victim of his own greedy impulses. Sabrina hated having to put them off, but she couldn't cash her reality check just yet.

"Not until I find out who's in the most trouble."

"That's easy." Mr. Kraft rounded the corner in front of her. He hugged his trusty clipboard to his chest. "You are. Unless you've got a darn good reason for roaming the halls without a pass."

"School hasn't started yet, Mr. Kraft."

"Exactly. Highly suspicious." The principal leaned toward her, scowling. "Sabotage is an expulsion offense."

"Believe me," Sabrina said honestly, "the *last* thing I want to do is ruin your chances for an A plus inspection from the school board."

"Then what are you doing here?"

"Going to the auto shop to see Harvey's new car," Sabrina explained. "Or rather old car. But it's new to him, so—"

"How old?" Mr. Kraft asked.

"Rusted, dented, doesn't run ancient."

"Really?" Mr. Kraft pulled out a pen and made a notation on the clipboard. "Mr. Grundel has made a hobby of restoring old cars ever since he fixed up his first old wreck at Westbridge. I think he'll be delighted to see that we're still carrying on that tradition."

"Cool! It's a Dodge—"

"Spare me the details." Mr. Kraft held up a hand, then checked the time. "The committee will be here in thirty minutes and I still haven't checked the science lab for stink bombs."

"Good luck. Gotta go!" Sabrina ducked around the corner and ran for the garage on the far side of the building.

Mr. Anderson hadn't arrived yet, and the garage shop was locked. Sabrina sat on the floor outside the door to wait and worry about her aunts. She was pretty sure that Aunt Zelda would choose her career, if given a choice between paying off Salem's on-line auction debt or saving her professional reputation. Aunt Hilda didn't want to lose the clock shop *or* the Grandfather Time Clock, but she couldn't keep both. The whole situation was so unfair.

If I had just gone out to celebrate after the Spelling Bee, my aunts wouldn't have been home when Mr. Hobson came to the door and Dr. Wadsworth called.

Sabrina brightened suddenly. If she used the reality check to change the past so they *had* gone out to party, *both* problems would be fixed!

"Two for one. Works for me!"

And Salem would benefit by default! If Aunt Zelda was in a restaurant eating Chinese, she wouldn't be alone with the cat when Florence's time-release spell kicked in and she lost her memory. So she wouldn't give Salem her credit card. No credit card, no temptation, no Internet auction buying spree.

I can save all three of them with a single reality change.

The only glitch was waiting to see what happened with Josh's A. I. Technologies stock and Mr. Kraft's school board inspection. And hope that Dreama kept her cool, which wouldn't be easy. It was just after eight, but the temperature was on a steady rise toward sizzling.

"Hi, Sabrina." Mr. Anderson inserted his key in the shop door. "You must be waiting for Harvey."

"Yeah. I'm a little curious about the car."

"Me, too." Mr. Anderson pushed the door open and flicked on the lights. "Come on in and have a seat."

Sabrina followed him inside and sat in a dented metal folding chair. "You don't happen to know how A. I. Technologies is doing on the stock market today, do you?"

"Nope. Not yet; the exchange isn't open yet." The slim, wiry shop teacher pulled a grease-stained pair of coveralls on over his regular clothes, then raised the garage bay door.

Sabrina looked at the clock on the wall. Eighty minutes to go before the stock exchange opened. When she had called Josh last night, he had shrugged off her concern about his investment. According to him, it was totally normal for people to get nervous when their hard-earned money was riding on the whims of a million other investors. He was so excited about being part of the Wall Street world that he had refused to listen to reason. Win or lose, he was on for the ride.

Feeling restless as the minutes slowly ticked by, Sabrina put her coffeehouse experience to good use. She set up the coffeemaker while Mr. Anderson cleared auto junk out of the bay to make room for the Kinkle clunker. When he was finished, the shop teacher went to a motorcycle standing against the back wall and began peeling masking tape off the newly painted wheel fenders.

"She's a beauty, isn't she?" Mr. Anderson beamed proudly and pulled a photo off the wall. He handed it to Sabrina. "This bike was a wreck when I brought it in six months ago. The guys did a great job."

"Wow!" Sabrina grinned as she stared at the *before* photo of the motorcycle. If the student mechanics did as well restoring the old Dodge, Harvey would end up with a dynamite car.

But it will be a makeover miracle, Sabrina thought as Brad pulled up, honking his horn. The rusted-out, rattling car he had in tow looked more like a broken-down nag than a classic, frisky Colt.

Harvey, however, was beaming as proudly as the shop teacher when he hopped out of the decrepit car. He stepped back as Brad steered away from the bay doors and positioned the patient for a rear end entry into the auto ER.

"Just take it slow!" Mr. Anderson called.

Hanging back, Sabrina crossed her fingers as Harvey signaled Brad to back up. When the back bumper of Brad's car touched the Colt, Harvey raised his hand for him to stop. He checked the front and rear bumpers of both cars to make sure they wouldn't hook, then waved Brad to back up again. Driving at a creeping crawl, Brad nudged the Colt toward the shop bay.

"Ah, we're just in time!" Wearing a nervous smile, Mr. Kraft entered the shop with the school board committee.

The two women wore expensive suits and stopped just inside the door. They exchanged a tolerant glance and clutched their bags close to minimize the risk of attracting stray specks of grease. The two men walked deeper into the garage with Mr. Kraft.

Rocking slightly, Mr. Kraft gave Harvey a curt wave. "Nice car, Mr. Kinkle."

The shorter man on the principal's right smiled and gave Harvey a thumbs-up.

That must be Mr. Grundel, Sabrina thought.

"Thanks!" Grinning, Harvey raised his hand to wave back.

Brad hit the brakes.

The Colt kept rolling. It lurched to a halt when the chain connecting the two cars went taut.

Before Sabrina finished exhaling with relief, Harvey jumped and frantically began to wave his hand around his head.

Brad gunned his car backward and hit the Colt. The old car shot toward the open bay door.

"No, no! It's a bee!" Harvey shouted, then remembered to raise his hand for a stop.

Brad slammed on the brakes again.

Sabrina raised her finger to stop the old car when it kept rolling. She froze just before she zinged off a point. She couldn't use her magic in front of Brad! He probably had the air-conditioning on in his car, which meant his witch-hunting gene had been activated in the colder environment. She couldn't be sure, but it wasn't worth the risk.

The Colt jerked when the chain tightened. This time the force snapped the weak link.

"Wait!" Unnerved when he realized the tow chain had broken, Harvey reacted instinctively. He yelled and shook his hand.

Reading that as the signal to back up, Brad rammed his car backward into the Colt, giving it a hefty shove.

"Look out!" the taller committeewoman cried out in alarm.

Mr. Kraft, Mr. Grundel, and the other man on the school board committee sprang aside.

Mr. Anderson stared in mute shock as the rusted runaway Colt zoomed into the bay and smashed into his motorcycle.

Sabrina's brain went numb for the next few seconds. She hadn't factored a car crash into her deliberations about how to spend the reality check.

All four members of the school board committee turned to glare at Mr. Kraft.

The blood drained from the principal's face.

Or a Kraft crisis, either!

"Nothing like this ever happened when *I* took auto shop at Westbridge," Mr. Grundel said.

"Don't you enforce standard safety procedures, Mr. Kraft?" the shorter woman asked.

"Uh-uh-well, uh-yes, Mrs. Sutton—usually," Mr. Kraft sputtered.

Brad leaped out of his car. "Is anyone hurt?"

Harvey dashed forward to inspect the damage to the old Colt. "This car was already a heap of junk, so it's kind of hard to tell."

Mr. Anderson fell on his knees before the motorcycle, which was squashed between the Colt and the wall. Air hissed out of the front tire, oil dripped from the crankcase, and the shiny frame was twisted. "You killed my bike."

"Gosh, I'm sorry, Mr. Anderson." Harvey looked sick. "I'll, uh, pay for the damages somehow."

"You shouldn't have to pay, Harvey," Brad said. "The accident happened on school property so the school's insurance will cover the damages."

"Is that true, Mr. Angelo?" the tall woman asked the thin man beside Mr. Grundel.

"I'm afraid so, Mrs. Markum." Mr. Angelo scowled at Harvey. "However, there's a five hundred dollar deductible, which we *will* expect you to pay, young man."

Harvey turned whiter than Mr. Kraft.

Five hundred dollars! Sabrina snapped out of her daze. That was all the money Harvey had. The money he needed to fix, register, and insure the Colt!

"That won't help the budget when the school's insurance premiums go sky high." Mrs. Sutton poked Mr. Kraft in the chest. "And it's all your fault."

"This inspection hasn't gotten off to a very good start, Mr. Kraft." A frosty smile split Mrs. Markum's face as she made a notation on a handheld electronic notebook.

Sabrina could feel Mr. Kraft's job slipping away. An image of the depressed, unshaven ex-principal lying on the sofa and channel surfing in the Spellman living room flashed through her mind. *No way!*

"Don't blame Mr. Kraft," Sabrina blurted out. "If I hadn't talked Harvey into getting the car, none of this would have happened."

"I might have known *you* had something to do with this!" Mr. Kraft fumed, than shriveled when Sabrina's desperate attempt to exonerate him was rejected.

"Irrelevant," Mr. Angelo said.

"Quite," Mrs. Sutton agreed.

"I'm ready to move on." Mr. Grundel took a last look at the motorcycle and heaved a sympathetic sigh for Mr. Anderson's loss.

"Is the air-conditioning broken, Mr. Kraft?" Mrs. Markum asked pointedly. "I get extremely cranky when it's too hot."

"Uh, no," Mr. Kraft coughed. "I'll call maintenance and have the problem resolved immediately."

So what's more important? Sabrina wondered as the principal led the inspection committee out the door. *Mr. Kraft's job, my happy home life, and Harvey's money? Or a clock, a career, and a zero balance on a credit card?*

It was impossible to make an objective choice, but sooner or later, she had to decide.

Chapter 8

Sabrina sat through her first class without hearing much of the discussion. Mr. Anderson had evicted her and Brad from the auto shop so he and Harvey could have a teacher-student "conference." Mr. Anderson was probably doing most of the talking. Besides, with Harvey and Mr. Kraft now on her growing list of needy reality change recipients, the effects of the Industrial Revolution on rural America wasn't compelling enough to hold Sabrina's attention.

The suffocating heat added discomfort to Sabrina's dismay. If Mr. Kraft had ordered the air-conditioning to be turned back on, it hadn't come up to speed yet. The sweat beads popping out on the neck of the student sitting in front of her was a disquieting reminder that Dreama was highly susceptible to magic malfunction during heat waves. Sabrina hadn't seen her friend in the halls before class. With luck, Dreama had decided to face truancy charges in the Other Realm rather than risk instant transformation into a mouse.

Sabrina decided to risk being late to second period so that she could track down Harvey. She found him leaning against his locker, staring into space.

"Harvey?" Sabrina moved her hand in front of his glazed eyes. He didn't even blink. She grabbed his arms and shook him. "Come on, Harvey! Snap out of it!"

No reaction.

Now he's catatonic as well as broke and busted for reckless parking!

"Please, Harvey," Sabrina pleaded.

"I got kicked out of auto shop," Harvey said in a dazed monotone.

Sabrina gasped. Harvey's whole guy identity was based on auto shop and being on the football team, even though he had only played once when a flu epidemic had benched most of the first string. Without car class, he wouldn't have *any* sense of direction! Not to mention that keeping his GPA high enough to get into college depended on the As he got in auto shop!

Harvey's prospects for the future had been flattened along with Mr. Anderson's motorcycle.

"I got kicked out of auto shop," Harvey said

again. His stunned gaze remained focused on the blank wall across the corridor.

"I can fix this, Harvey." Sabrina gently turned his head toward her. "I'm not kidding. I really can."

If she changed things so Harvey turned down his uncle's car, there wouldn't be a shop accident for the school board committee to witness! Then Mr. Kraft's job wouldn't be in terrible jeopardy, either. *Another two-fer!*

Sabrina dreaded the thought of turning down her aunts' request for a reality quick fix, but Harvey's situation was infinitely more dire than theirs. He had fewer options and a life span of only eight or nine decades. Her aunts had centuries ahead of them. In another hundred years, nobody would care that Aunt Zelda's scientific rep had been temporarily tainted, and she could afford to pay off Salem's credit card debt, even if she didn't want to. Aunt Hilda would have gotten tired of running a clock shop in another fifty years anyway.

It wasn't like they had committed a major crime or lost their magical powers or anything.

Hilda grunted as she dropped the large carton on the clock shop counter, then glanced back as Zelda carried Salem inside. Zelda hadn't been able to stop payment on the cat's credit card purchases or deactivate the card at Bid-and-Buy. She had brought the laptop with her to keep trying. However, since Salem had no willpower and could access the on-line auction site through the desktop computer in the study, they had brought him, too.

"This better be good, Salem," Hilda said.

"It is!" The cat leaped out of Zelda's arm and onto the box that had been delivered right before they left the house.

"For two hundred and forty-seven dollars it better be!" Zelda set the laptop down and connected it to the shop phone line.

"If that's all it costs to save the Grandfather Time Clock, we'll be getting off cheap." Hilda reached behind the counter for a cutter. Salem wouldn't tell them what was in the box, but he was certain Mr. Hobson would jump at the chance to own it instead of the priceless Other Realm antique.

Zelda and Salem tensed with anticipation as Hilda sliced through the sealing tape and opened the carton flaps.

"Another clock?" Hilda pulled the timepiece out of the box and ran her fingers over the carved raven-wood frame. The face numbers were engraved in old Celtic script.

"I like the Irish design," Zelda said, "but I seriously doubt Mr. Hobson will want this instead of the Grandfather Time Clock."

"This isn't *just* a clock," Salem said defensively. "It's a Screaming Banshee wake-up alarm and intruder alert. Go ahead, Hilda. Set the alarm to go off in ten minutes."

"Humor him, Hilda." Zelda flipped open the laptop and signed on to the Internet. "It might be good for a laugh."

"Which I need as much as we need another clock," Hilda grumbled. She set the alarm for ten-fifteen and set the clock aside when Mr. Hobson knocked on the door. "Any last words before I let the mortal in, Salem?"

"No. Guess I'll take my morning nap." Yawning, Salem jumped to the table in the middle of the floor. He curled up around a silver column clock that displayed four global time zones.

"Good morning, ladies!" Mr. Hobson smiled.

"You're in a good mood," Hilda said. "What's wrong?"

"I can't wait to get started so I can get this inventory done and take my beautiful grandfather clock home." The appraiser flung his jacket over the counter and rolled up his sleeves. "Now, if you'll excuse me—"

Zelda intercepted him at the storeroom door. "Before you make a final decision, Mr. Hobson, you might want to reconsider your choice. We just got this fabulous clock and security alarm piece in this morning."

Mr. Hobson cast a cursory glance at the Celtic clock, then brushed past Zelda. "No, thanks."

"Guess that settles that." Hilda picked up an elegant crystal clock and sighed. "We've got to tell him it's no deal."

Zelda nodded. "No deal, no appraisal, no insurance renewal, no business license, no clock shop."

"Unless we cash in some of our Other Realm stocks," Hilda suggested hopefully. "PotionsToGo. spell is at an all-time high."

"And still going up." Zelda shook her head. "No. We decided the shop had to make or break it on its own."

"Then there's no point putting this off." Hilda squared her shoulders and strode toward the storeroom. Just as she got to the door, a shrill shriek reverberated through the shop. "Has it been ten minutes already?"

"Wow!" Salem sat up. "If I was breaking in, that banshee cry would scare me away."

"Salem!" Zelda said sharply. "No talking! Mr. Hobson might hear you."

Mr. Hobson called out from the storeroom. "I *love* that clock!"

Hilda popped her head in. "You can't have it." She shrugged. "Sorry, but—"

Another bloodcurdling wail cut her off.

"Bansheeeee!" Salem leaped to the counter to check out the screaming clock. "Hey! It's only ten-thirteen."

Mr. Hobson glared at Hilda. "We had a deal!"

Hilda ignored him to look back at the Screaming Banshee Alarm Clock. "Well, either it doesn't keep accurate time or we've got company."

"We've been raided!" Zelda came back out of the

back room with her hands in the air. Two Other Realm uniformed cops followed her. Three more popped in behind Hilda.

"Whatever it is, I didn't do it!" Salem dove for cover under the counter.

Mr. Hobson stared at the cat and then at the cops. He folded his arms with a weary sigh. "Are these gentlemen figments of my imagination, too?"

"I wish," Hilda muttered.

Officer Peccadillo, a robust, red-faced man with bushy eyebrows, stepped forward and flashed his badge. "Hilda Spellman, you're under arrest for endangering priceless Other Realm property, utilizing that property for personal gain in the mortal world, and being derelict in your duty as a duly appointed trustee of Time, Etc., Unlimited."

Hilda gasped. If she was convicted, she could lose her powers for life! Not to mention having chronic dishpan hands after fifty years of scrubbing baked-on baby potions off cauldrons at the Little Witch Preschool. "What are you being charged with, Zelda?"

"All of the above *plus* exceeding the twenty-four-hour magical mayhem in the mortal world limit." Zelda winced as another officer pointed her into handcuffs.

"But we weren't *really* going to give Mr. Hobson the Grandfather Time Clock!" Hilda protested.

"Tell it to the judge." Officer Peccadillo zapped her into handcuffs, too.

"What about our deal?" Mr. Hobson blustered. "That's my clock!"

"Sorry, sir," Officer Peccadillo said, "but the Grandfather Time Clock is being confiscated."

"Well, fine!" Fuming, the appraiser yanked his jacket off the counter and stormed out the door. "No clock, no inventory!"

"Well, that's just great," Hilda said. "We're going to lose our powers and the clock shop!"

When Salem realized that the shop had suddenly gone quiet, he peeked over the top of the counter. "Hello?"

Hilda, Zelda, the clock guy, and the cops were gone.

"Oh, no! I've been abandoned in a clock shop! No water. No food! And nobody knows I'm here!"

Salem started to sob, then quickly pulled himself together. Crying wasn't going to solve his problem or help Hilda and Zelda. They were on a fast track to a quick trial. Maybe in Judge "Stiff Sentence" Stone's court. Salem had gotten the usual one hundred years as a cat for the crime of trying to conquer the mortal world, but Hilda and Zelda could be facing life sentences as mortals! And the Witches' Council wouldn't let a warlock who was doing time as a cat live with mortals.

"I don't want another family! I want—" Salem stopped wailing. "Sabrina!"

Sabrina could fix everything, if she knew what

had happened. The school had to deliver a message about a family emergency.

Salem padded across the counter to the phone and pushed the receiver off the hook. Instead of a dial tone, he heard the wavering hiss and hoot of a modem connection. Another oh, no! Zelda's computer was still on-line! He could shut down the Internet connection, but he couldn't switch the phone cord from the laptop back to the phone with paws!

"Stay calm. There's got to be another way. You're a smart cat. Think!"

Salem blinked.

SmartCat!

"That's it!" Salem raced back across the counter to the laptop and did a quick search for Westbridge High. The school even had a one-click, contact us, e-mail address! He put a paw on the keyboard, and typed a message.

Please, deliver to Sabrina Spellman: Emergency! Extremely urgent! Family crisis at the clock shop. Hurry! Salem.

He hit Send, then sat back.

He had no idea how long it would take before someone at Westbridge High read the e-mail and passed it on to Sabrina. He was hungry. And locked in a store with nothing to eat and nothing to do.

The clocks ticked, hummed, whirred, and bonged.

Salem wished he had the pocket-sized TV, cell phone, and calculator he had been bidding on. Then he could pass the time watching TV or calling radio talk shows or figuring out how much to charge for Wacky Wonder Water Zoom rides so he could pay off Zelda's credit card debt in less than twenty-five years.

His gaze flicked to the laptop.

When Sabrina cashed the reality check to save her aunts, anything he did now would be changed, too.

"I wonder what BargainHound is bidding on now," Salem purred as he logged on to Bid-and-Buy. "Look out, pooch. The cat is back!"

Harvey didn't begin to recover from his identity meltdown until Sabrina dragged him toward the cafeteria and said the magic word. "Lunch."

He stopped, blinked, and shook his head. "Hungry."

"A new word! That's a good sign." Sabrina let go of his hand. Harvey had a low-key personality to begin with, but his zombie-like trance and one-sentence monologue were wearing on her nerves. She would have cashed the reality check right away, but she wanted to check with her aunts first. She couldn't shake the nagging suspicion that there was a critical catch they hadn't mentioned.

"Food." Harvey started down the hall, following his nose toward the aromas of low-cost fried stuff wafting from the cafeteria.

Sabrina ran interference so Harvey didn't knock anyone down in his single-minded quest for sustenance. She tried to hurry him along when Mr. Kraft and the inspection committee fell into formation behind them. Harvey was stuck in low gear, and Mr. Kraft gave them a scathing look as he steered the committee around them.

Mrs. Markum rubbed her arms and shivered. "Is the thermostat broken, Mr. Kraft? Now it's freezing in here."

"I'll have maintenance adjust the settings as soon as we finish touring the cafeteria." Mr. Kraft's jaw flexed under a strained smile.

It *was* colder than usual, Sabrina realized. Brad's magic sensors were functioning again, but Dreama was a no-show. *A major relief,* she thought as the adults moved ahead. Even without the heat factor, the inept Other Realm witch was in the spell-casting high-risk pool.

"The school is remarkably clean, though," Mrs. Sutton said.

"Which brings the complaint to compliment ratio up to roughly twenty to one," the principal murmured.

Mr. Angelo frowned. "You haven't gone over budget on maintenance costs, have you?"

"No, not at all." Mr. Kraft stiffened. "I run a tight ship and the students cooperate—or else."

Sabrina didn't feel sorry for him. If not for her personal stake regarding Mr. Kraft's employment status, his dismissal would be a relief. However, she'd settle for watching him squirm under the committee's merciless scrutiny.

"Food." Harvey quickened his pace as Mr. Kraft and entourage turned the corner into the cafeteria.

The sound of chanting sent a chill up Sabrina's spine.

"Fire Mr. Kraft. Fire Mr. Kraft."

Mrs. Markum's outraged voice rose above the ominous chorus. "What is the meaning of this?"

Sabrina dashed into the cafeteria ahead of Harvey and froze. Except for Brad, who was seated and calmly chewing on a chicken leg, no one was eating. Across the room, Dreama stood at the front of a student protest group holding a sign that read: Down with Tyranny at Westbridge High!

Her followers continued to chant and shake signs with similar slogans: No More Forced Labor!

Detention, Not Slavery!

Harvey made a hard left toward the food line.

"Fire Mr. Kraft. Fire Mr. Kraft."

Furious, the principal stomped toward the assembly. "Put those signs away and get back to your classes!"

The protestors ignored him.

"Fire Mr. Kraft. Fire Mr. Kraft."

Sabrina rushed up to Dreama. "What are you doing?"

The school board committee closed in.

"She's disrupting the orderly function of this school, that's what," Mr. Kraft sputtered.

"That much is obvious," Mrs. Sutton said. "I want to know why."

Dreama held up a hand to quiet the crowd. "Well, originally I was going to protest the no air-conditioning policy."

"Are you saying Mr. Kraft *deliberately* turned off the air in this sweltering heat?" Mr. Grundel asked, aghast.

Dreama nodded.

"But he only did it to impress you!" For the second time in a matter of hours, Sabrina rushed to Mr. Kraft's defense, a weird but futile twist of fate. "And the air's back on!"

"Right." Dreama shrugged. "So since we were already organized, we decided to protest being forced to clean the school building yesterday instead."

"You weren't forced. You all had a choice!" Mr. Kraft countered. "Clean or serve your detentions."

Dreama's dark eyes flashed. "But you gave *everyone* detention for no reason. Not good ones, anyway."

"Well!" Mrs. Markum turned and whispered to her fellow committee members. Her face was set with firm resolve when she looked up. "Under the circumstances, Mr. Kraft, we have no choice but to terminate you immediately."

Mr. Kraft began to hyperventilate.

Dreama was so exuberant over the success of her

student rally that she forgot where she was and tugged a victory celebration before Sabrina could stop her.

Horns blared. Colorful confetti and balloons rained from the ceiling. Paper hats appeared on startled heads, and hands suddenly held noisemakers.

"What was that?" Brad leaped out of his chair, his hard gaze scanning the crowd. He zeroed in on Dreama. "You! You used magic! You're—a witch!"

"Oops!" Dreama winced, then instantly shrank and morphed into a furry, brown mouse.

Everyone gasped.

Mrs. Sutton fainted.

"Cool!" Brad grinned.

Realizing the situation was totally out of control, Sabrina scooped Dreama off the floor and tucked the mouse into the side pocket of her bag as she ran out. Alone in the corridor, she dropped to the floor and pulled a pen and the reality check from the middle compartment of her bag. She had to sign it *now*. An unexpected catch couldn't possibly make things any worse than they already were.

Sabrina flipped the check over and gripped the pen.

Chapter 9

"What's keeping Sabrina?" Zelda paced in the holding cell at the Other Realm Police Headquarters. "Salem must be trying to contact her."

"That's for sure." Hilda shifted on the uncomfortable bunk. "There's nothing to eat in the shop."

Zelda slapped her forehead. "The phone isn't working! I left the computer connected."

"Wait!" Hilda sat up. "We get one phone call, right?"

"I think so." Zelda looked around the small, dingy cell with dismay. "I've never been arrested for a major crime before."

"Well, I'm sure we do, and we can use it to call the school." Hilda stood up and went to the bars. "Hey! Yoo-hoo! Somebody!"

Officer Peccadillo popped in, holding half a sandwich. "What? I'm on my lunch break."

"Where's our lunch?" Hilda asked.

"You don't have time to eat." The officer checked his watch. "You go before Judge Stone in twenty minutes."

"On an empty stomach? I don't think so." Hilda pointed. Nothing happened. "What's wrong with my finger?"

"Your powers have been suspended pending the outcome of the trial. Standard procedure for serious offenders." The officer took a bite of his sandwich and waved as he prepared to pop out.

"Not so fast!" Zelda jumped forward. "We want to call our niece."

Peccadillo swallowed. "Is that an out-of-Realm call?"

"Yes, but I'll pay for it," Zelda pleaded. "We have to contact Sabrina as soon as possible."

"Is she your lawyer?" the officer asked.

"Better," Hilda said. "She's got a reality check, and we have to reach her before she cashes it to change something else."

"It's a matter of magic or no magic," Zelda added.

"I shouldn't do this, but you're in so much trouble a reality check is the *only* thing that can get you out of it." The officer pointed, and a pay phone appeared on the wall. "There's your cell phone."

"Thank you." Zelda picked up the receiver, dialed

the operator, and entered her calling card number. "Westbridge High School. In Massachusetts."

"That was a joke." Peccadillo eyed Hilda with a boyish grin. *"Cell* phone. Get it?"

Hilda didn't crack a smile. "I got it, but laughing is what got us into this mess."

Zelda didn't laugh, either. She held the phone out so Hilda could hear the recorded message.

"Sorry. All circuits are busy. Please try again later."

Sabrina popped into the alley behind Hickory Dickery Clock just in case the appraiser was still inside working on the inventory. She had realized that she didn't know how to cash the reality check after it was signed, and she had tried to call her aunts for instructions. Every phone in the school had been mobbed with excited kids and hysterical teachers. It wasn't every day that party paraphernalia appeared out of thin air or a student was changed into a rodent. She had prudently ducked into the rest room before transporting to avoid Brad.

Dreama stuck her furry little head out of Sabrina's bag and squeaked.

"Be patient, Dreama. I've got a plan."

Sabrina pushed the mouse and the reality check back into her bag and walked to the front door. The Closed for Inventory sign was hanging in the window, and the door was locked. She didn't see anyone inside and used a quick point to spring the lock.

"Aunt Hilda! Aunt Zelda!"

"It's about time!" Salem's head appeared over the laptop screen on the counter. "I sent that e-mail over two hours ago!"

"What e-mail?" Sabrina dropped her bag on the display table in the middle of the room.

"The one I sent to you care of Westbridge High." The cat's nose twitched. "I smell mouse."

Dreama crawled out of the side pouch and perched on the top of Sabrina's bag.

"I see mouse!"

"Forget it, Salem," Sabrina warned. "That's Dreama. Off-limits."

"Oh." The cat sagged. "Couldn't I just chase her a little? I've been spending so much time in front of this computer lately, I'm not getting enough exercise."

"Nice try, but no way." Sabrina craned her neck to peer into the back room. Her aunts weren't there. Neither was the Grandfather Time Clock. Maybe they had gone to rescue it from Mr. Hobson. "Are you on-line? How's A. I. Technologies doing in the stock market?"

Salem hit a few keys. "It's up by eighteen points."

"Well, at least something's going right." Sabrina mentally crossed Josh off her reality check short list and looked at the cat askance. "Are you bidding at that auction site again?"

"Yes, I am," Salem grinned. "I just booked the

Emperor's Suite in the Space Hotel for the grand opening in 2017. We'll have a whole week in orbital paradise for a measly five million dollars."

"What? You can't put five million dollars on Aunt Zelda's credit card!"

"It's not like the deal is permanent," Salem huffed. "As soon as you cash the reality check to get Zelda and Hilda out of jail, there won't be a deal because I won't be locked in the clock shop starving with nothing to do."

"Jail?" Sabrina gawked at the cat. "Aunt Hilda and Aunt Zelda are in jail? For what?"

"Endangering the Grandfather Time Clock and creating magical mayhem. That's why I sent you an e-mail," Salem said. "To tell you there was a family emergency."

"I didn't get an e-mail!"

Mr. Kraft burst through the front door. Wild-eyed and frantic, with flyaway hair and askew tie, he looked totally crazed. "Where's my Zuzu? What's the emergency? Is she okay?" He halted and collected himself to fix Sabrina with a practiced stare of authority. "Why aren't you in school?"

"Uh—" Sabrina's head was spinning. Everything was falling apart too fast. "Why aren't you?"

"Because *I* was fired and escorted off the premises," Mr. Kraft snapped. "What's your excuse?"

"A family emergency?" Sabrina smiled lamely.

"Oh, right." Mr. Kraft nodded. "That's what the

e-mail said . . . which *you* didn't get because I did. So how did you know your aunt was in trouble? And who's Salem?"

"I am." Salem waved a paw.

"A talking cat," Mr. Kraft said with a deadpan expression. "That sends e-mail."

The mouse charged across the table at Mr. Kraft, squeaking in fury. Dreama halted at the edge of the table, sat up, and shook her tiny front paws.

Mr. Kraft arched an eyebrow. "And I'm being chewed out by an enraged mouse that used to be a girl."

Unable to resist his feline impulses, Salem leaped onto the table and slammed a paw down on Dreama's tail.

Sabrina had to think, and she couldn't do it while everyone was running amok. She grabbed Salem by the scruff of the neck and picked up the mouse. "Behave or you'll both be confined in a cat carrier and a mouse cage as fast as I can point. Do we understand each other?"

The cat and mouse nodded, and Sabrina released them on the table.

"I think I need to sit down," Mr. Kraft murmured as he swayed.

"Please do." Sabrina pointed up two comfortable Queen Anne chairs and collapsed in one of them.

Mr. Kraft kicked the legs and pushed on the cushion of the second chair. When he was convinced it wasn't an illusion, he sat down.

"Okay." Sabrina took a deep breath. "Everyone I know is in serious trouble."

Dreama squeaked and hung her little head.

"That's the understatement of the day," Salem said.

"I'll say. I've lost my job, my self-respect, *and* my mind," Mr. Kraft sighed.

"Big deal," Salem scoffed. "Zuzu and Hilda could lose their *powers*. Forever."

"And I've only got *one* reality check." Sabrina threw up her hands in frustration.

"So?" Salem asked with a touch of impertinence.

"So I can avert disaster for you, Aunt Hilda, and Aunt Zelda by going out to celebrate after the Spelling Bee instead of staying home."

Salem cocked his head to consider that, then nodded. "That would do it. Just endorse the check and they'll never see the inside of the slammer."

"Zuzu's in jail?" Mr. Kraft slapped his hand to his face.

"Only until I cash my reality check," Sabrina reassured him. "But if I do that, then I won't be able to help Harvey and Dreama and—I can't believe I'm saying this—you, Mr. Kraft. And it's my fault you're all in trouble."

"I knew it!" Mr. Kraft slammed his fist into the palm of his other hand.

"How do you figure that?" Salem asked.

Dreama squeaked.

Sabrina quickly explained that because she had

the reality check and the ability to change the past, she had talked Harvey into taking his uncle's old car. "He was going to turn it down until I opened my big mouth."

"And if Kinkle's miserable old wreck hadn't crashed while the inspection committee was in the auto shop, *I'd* still have a job."

Dreama sat up on her haunches and squeaked frantically.

"The car crash wasn't the only factor, Mr. Kraft," Sabrina said. "Dreama formed her protest group because you turned off the air-conditioning."

"So?" Mr. Kraft asked, mimicking Salem's impertinent tone.

Sabrina sighed. The various cause-and-effect factors were too confusing to explain in detail. "So if I didn't have the reality check, I might have tried to convince you that turning off the air was a bad idea. And then the chain of events that led up to Brad outing Dreama as a witch wouldn't have happened and she wouldn't be a mouse."

"I have a headache." Mr. Kraft rubbed his temples.

"Don't worry, Mr. Kraft," Sabrina shrugged. "If I can figure out what event to change so none of these things happen, this conversation isn't happening, either."

Mr. Kraft nodded. "Under the circumstances, that makes perfect sense."

Sabrina sighed. "I wish I'd never won the reality check in the first place."

Dreama squeaked and jumped up and down.

"That's it!" Salem sat bolt upright. "If you lose the Spelling Bee, *everything* will change!"

Sabrina started, then nodded slowly. "You're right, Salem. It's the only solution. If Agatha wins, Florence and Charlene won't ambush Aunt Hilda and Aunt Zelda with time-release spells."

"And you won't make any decisions based on being able to alter the past because you won't have a reality check," Salem finished.

Dreama vigorously thumped her tail.

Sabrina jumped up. The only downside to the plan was that Aunt Hilda and Aunt Zelda would still be humiliated and harassed by Florence and Charlene at Other Realm social functions because another Spellman had lost the Spelling Bee to another MacFadden. A small price to pay.

"It's time to sign!"

Hilda nervously shifted from one foot to the other. Officer Peccadillo had taken her and Zelda to the courtroom early so they could confer with the public defender appointed to represent them. They had been waiting in the defendants' box five minutes, and the trial was about to start. The Rule Bearer appeared and positioned her stool in front of the judge's stand, but there was still no sign of their lawyer.

"Why are we still here?" Zelda had chewed the nails on her left hand down to the quick. She started gnawing on the index finger of her right hand.

Hilda pulled Zelda's hand down. "That's your pointing finger!"

"My *deactivated* pointing finger." Zelda crossed her arms and tucked both hands under them.

Hilda understood her sister's anxiety. To keep herself from going nuts, she had decided to assume that Sabrina was just delayed and hadn't forsaken them. Believing their present circumstances might *not* happen made coping a lot easier.

A young man carrying a bulging briefcase rushed in from the misty ether. He had papers clenched in his teeth, and he struggled to slip on his jacket as he ran. His briefcase popped open when he dropped it.

"Our public defender is here," Hilda said.

Zelda watched as the young man scrambled on his hands and knees to collect his files. "We're in trouble."

"You noticed." Hilda refused to be upset when the young man stumbled to the railing. She was certain that any minute now they would be instantly transported back to a point in time where a single change would eliminate criminal activities from their future.

The young man finished shrugging into his suit coat and took the papers out of his mouth. "Hilda Spellman? Zelda Spellman?"

Hilda smiled. "I'm Hilda."

"Ah!" His eyes lit up as he glanced at Zelda. "Then you must be Zelda."

"A brilliant deduction." Zelda eyed him coldly. "You're late."

"Uh . . . yes, but I just got your case file a minute ago." He stuck out his hand. "Sherman Coots, at your service."

The Rule Bearer stepped onto her stool and pushed the feather dangling from her cap out of her eyes. "Hear ye! Hear ye!"

Sherman stepped toward the barrister's table in front of the prisoner box, then stepped back and whispered. "What are you in for?"

Hilda and Zelda exchanged glances.

"You've got thirty seconds to read the file," Hilda whispered back. Judge Stone wouldn't appreciate a client-attorney conference disrupting his grand entrance, and she didn't want contempt added to the list of charges.

"All rise!" The Rule Bearer straightened her vest.

A stooped, elderly man in black robes and a massive, white, powdered wig entered through a door surrounded by mist. He slowly climbed the stairs to his high-backed, leather chair.

Zelda leaned toward Hilda. "I just had a horrible thought."

"I can't imagine why," Hilda hissed through gritted teeth.

The judge banged his gavel.

"Court is in session, the Honorable Judge Stone

presiding." The Rule Bearer hopped off her stool, tucked it under her arm, and left.

"What if Sabrina has inadvertently created a repeating time loop?" Zelda asked.

The judge turned his stony gaze on the prisoners. "No bail!"

"I object!" Sherman leaped to his feet.

"Overruled!" The judge smiled and banged his gavel again.

Sherman shrugged and took his seat.

Hilda's eyes widened as the implications of what Zelda had just said hit her. Although everyone else's memories would be erased when the reality check shifted time, Sabrina would remember everything that had transpired in the current reality when she went back. She would arrive in the past a few minutes *before* the event she had decided to change happened. However, once the designated event-moment *passed,* Sabrina would forget everything that had happened in this previous reality, too.

It wasn't likely, but if Sabrina failed to make the proper change, the whole awful sequence of events they had just experienced would play out exactly the same.

Except Sabrina wouldn't *know* the events were identical or that the original timeline would *keep* repeating itself until she made the necessary alteration.

If she ever did.

People had a tendency to react to certain things

for the same reasons the same way most of the time.

Hilda suddenly had a clearer understanding of why the Witches' Council rarely issued a reality check. The accounting department of Time, Etc., Unlimited might never get the potentially endless overlapping, converging, and diverging timelines unraveled.

Just *thinking* about it made her head hurt.

Hilda turned to Zelda with a gasp. "Has the Witches' Council ever put a stop payment on a reality check?"

Chapter 10

☆

Zelda's attention was drawn back to the trial when Judge Stone finished reading the charges.

"How do your clients plead, Mr. Coots?" Judge Stone yawned.

"Guilty, Your Honor," Sherman said.

"I object!" Hilda shouted.

Zelda threw her hand over Hilda's mouth. "Objection withdrawn."

"You're too late. You're *both* in contempt!" The judge laughed. "That's ten more years of Pre-School pot-scrubbing when you're convicted. And you will be con—what's that?" The judge pointed his gavel toward the swirling mists surrounding the courtroom.

Zelda turned to see the time-ripple rolling toward her out of the ether, and she grabbed onto Hilda's arm. Sabrina had deposited the check, and the time shift was in process. "Here we go!"

"Thank goodness!" Hilda stuck her tongue out at the judge.

"I object!" The judge shouted and pounded his desk with the gavel. "Order in the Court!"

"The defense rests!" Sherman wiped his brow and sagged with relief.

Zelda squeezed her eyes closed as the time-ripple washed over the court.

WHOOOSHHHHHHH!

"He's out!" Hilda whistled and applauded when Tinker Bottoms failed to successfully execute a controlled cleaning cyclone spell.

"Shhh." Zelda held a finger to her mouth, but she was thrilled, too. Tinker's little whirlwind had rampaged through the amphitheater, ripping up seats and flinging spectators instead of sweeping down the main aisle picking up litter.

"That was exciting!" Salem smoothed his ruffled fur with his paw.

"Yes! Agatha and Sabrina are the only ones left." Hilda crossed her fingers in her lap.

Zelda nodded. After all these centuries, the Spellman family finally had a chance to beat the Mac-Faddens in the Annual Spelling Bee. When she caught Sabrina staring at her, she grinned and held up two thumbs to show her faith and support.

Sabrina returned Aunt Zelda's thumbs-up and

hoped her aunts read her pained expression as a nervous smile. They weren't making this any easier. But then, as Salem had pointed out before she'd endorsed the reality check, *they* didn't have any recollection of the old timeline. No one remembered—except her.

At least the time-shift process had gone smoothly. When the time-ripple hit, she had been swept back to a few minutes before the event she had noted on the check's memo line: casting the fountain-of-truth spell Drell was just about to announce.

Still looking magnificently ridiculous in his flowing wizard robes and pointed hat, Drell waited until Tinker Bottoms trudged off the stage. Then he reached into the cauldron on the judges' table. "Sabrina Spellman, a fountain-of-truth spell."

"Like *that's* a surprise," Sabrina muttered as she walked to center stage. She and Agatha MacFadden were the only two contestants left in the Other Realm Annual Spelling Bee for newly licensed card-carrying witches. When she *failed* to cast a working fountain-of-truth spell this time, she'd be out of the competition.

Then Harvey wouldn't have an identity crisis, Mr. Kraft wouldn't lose his job, Dreama wouldn't be a mouse, and her aunts wouldn't be arrested. Since having the reality check hadn't influenced her conversation with Josh, she was pretty sure he'd still buy his stock. She hoped so anyway, because

AITE was rising in value. In spite of his protests to the contrary, Salem didn't remember and wouldn't miss the Wacky Wonder Water Zoom—whatever *that* was!

A tense hush settled over the audience seated in the amphitheater on the summit of Cloud Nine Mountain when Sabrina turned to face them. She was acutely aware that the arrogant and extremely annoying Agatha was staring at her. That wasn't as hard to take as her aunts' hopeful attention.

Aunt Hilda and Aunt Zelda were sitting in the front row just like before. Their smiles were fixed around gritted teeth, and they both had their fingers crossed.

Salem lounged in the seat between them. "Why don't they ever ask them to cast a turn-the-cat-back-into-a-warlock spell?"

"To keep the world safe from maniacal monarchs out to corner the global tuna market." Zelda scowled the cat into silence.

Sabrina looked away from her guardians as she limbered up her pointing finger with a few knuckle bends. Her aunts would be totally devastated when she lost the Spelling Bee, but she didn't have any choice.

"What's the matter, Sabrina?" Agatha MacFadden's sarcastic tone sliced through the quiet. "Nervous?"

Like I'm not under enough pressure! Sabrina's anxiety intensified as she turned to stare at the smug, young witch waiting on the sidelines. Condescending conceit was definitely a MacFadden family trait.

Sabrina really hated the idea of losing to the obnoxious witch. She despised Agatha's aunts, too. If it weren't for Florence and Charlene, Aunt Hilda and Aunt Zelda couldn't have talked her into participating in the traditional spectacle of dueling spells to begin with! But they had looked so *pathetic* when they had begged that she hadn't been able to refuse. It wasn't just because they had both lost to a MacFadden when they had competed in the Spelling Bee centuries before. Florence and Charlene teased them about their resounding defeats every chance they got.

Sabrina smiled at Agatha. "Just warming up."

Agatha rolled brilliant blue eyes and flipped her long, dark hair over her shoulder.

Sabrina started. *Just warming up.* Those were the same words she had used the first time around! The realization shook her. What if the past had a stubborn streak and resisted being changed? Or what if she was so susceptible to specific responses she couldn't alter her actions?

"Whenever you're ready, Sabrina." Drell frowned from his seat at the judges' table. "Preferably before the end of the *next* millennium."

Agatha smirked.

Beware, Sabrina cautioned herself.

"Right. One truth spell coming up." Sabrina graced the judges with a tight smile, then turned to the audience. She had to give the impression she was looking for a suitable victim even if her choice didn't matter.

As long as I don't choose Charlene MacFadden.

Sabrina scanned the curious faces watching her. When the spectators decided to attend the Spelling Bee, they automatically volunteered to be subjects of spells that required them. The contestant's spells weren't sealed, but they remained active until the competition was over—whether the magic worked or not. At the moment, the audience contained a giant toadstool, a witch with smoking ears, several people with bumps and bruises inflicted by the cyclone, and something that resembled a dehydrated swamp creature. Fortunately, the contestants weren't held accountable for the spells that went awry.

Sabrina winced. She had had similar thoughts about how the Spelling Bee worked the last time, too. Like her retort to Agatha, the mental response had *felt* right. Fighting her natural impulses was almost impossible. Cashing the reality check to solve everyone's problems was obviously *not* going to be a snap.

Taking a deep breath, Sabrina raised her finger to randomly select a subject for the fountain-of-truth spell.

Anyone but Charlene MacFadden, she told herself again to lock in the deviation.

"Take your time, Sabrina!" Florence MacFadden, a thin woman with straight brown hair and beady eyes set in a pinched face, chuckled softly and nudged her sister.

"You're not the first Spellman to suffer from stage fright, dear." Shorter and rounder than Florence, Charlene MacFadden glanced down the front row at Hilda.

Hilda stiffened and glared back. "I did *not* have stage fright! You put a mute-and-freeze hex on me, Charlene!"

Sabrina's gaze shifted from Charlene to Hilda. Aunt Hilda had become too petrified and choked to speak in her final Spelling Bee round with Charlene.

"That's *still* a lame excuse, Hilda." Charlene sighed and fluffed her curly red hair.

Sabrina flexed her finger and forced her gaze to settle on a handsome, older warlock with gray hair and a twinkle in his eyes. He caught her staring and pointed himself into knight's armor. Startled, Sabrina looked away.

Hilda raised her finger to zap Charlene.

Zelda grabbed Hilda's hand and shook her head.

This is so unfair! Sabrina glared at Charlene. She was positive Charlene had sabotaged Aunt Hilda with a spell during the final round of their Spelling Bee and suspected Florence had used similar tactics on Zelda. Aunt Zelda had lost to Florence when she had become tongue-tied and none of her words had made sense. That was bad enough, but the MacFadden sisters hadn't been satisfied with their ill-gotten victories. They had compounded the injustice with their relentless taunts over the centuries.

Aunt Hilda and Aunt Zelda had been forced to take it—until they had decided to spare themselves by skipping Other Realm social functions.

Avenging the Spellman family honor suddenly seemed like a dynamite idea.

Sabrina raised her finger to strike back.

"Powered by the magic mountain,
truth flows from the hanging fountain."

Sabrina snapped a point at Charlene. Her eyes widened as a small, ornately carved mini-fountain appeared above the witch's head.

Uh-oh! She had given in to her lust for vengeance and zapped Charlene again!

The startled witch squealed as sparkling bursts of light overflowed the fountain bowl and fell on her head and shoulders. "No fair!"

"Foul!" Florence brushed sparkles off her shoulder, then leaned back out of range.

Hilda grinned. "All's fair in love, war, and the Spelling Bee, Charlene. I've heard you say it a hundred times."

"At least," Zelda nodded.

Sabrina's mind raced. The MacFadden sisters had cheated her aunts, but there was no proof. She hesitated, torn between exposing Charlene or making sure the disastrous timeline was changed.

Beads of cold sweat broke out on Sabrina's neck and brow. The instant she finished the spell, she wouldn't remember *anything* that had occurred in the old reality. Even though she *knew* what was at stake now, she had repeated most of what had happened before anyway.

Charlene glowered with defiant eyes, daring her.

Aunt Hilda and Aunt Zelda leaned forward with hopeful intensity.

Sabrina tried to stay focused on her mission. If she didn't complete the spell, she'd lose the Spelling Bee, and the awful future would change.

And the horrible MacFaddens would win—again.

But her aunts were counting on her to reclaim the Spellman family's honor. She just couldn't let them down.

Maybe I won't make the same mistakes because I have the reality check this time!

Sabrina smiled.

She didn't *need* to remember the horrible chain of events that had gotten her family and friends into so much trouble. If she had the reality check and everything went wrong again, she could come back to fix things again, too!

She raised her finger.

*"In your zeal my aunt to beat,
did you, Charlene MacFadden, cheat?"*

Sabrina pointed at Charlene.
WHOOOOSSHHHHHHH!

Chapter 11

Sabrina swayed and shook the dizziness out of her head. She winced as she awaited the result of the truth spell she had cast on Charlene MacFadden. She desperately wanted to beat Agatha MacFadden *and* avenge the wrongs done to her aunts.

"Of course, I cheated!" Charlene's eyes bulged as the truth poured out of her mouth. "It was the only way I could win!"

Wahoo! A wave of relief washed over Sabrina. Even if Agatha ended up winning this Spelling Bee, everyone in the Other Realm now knew that her aunts had been robbed when they had competed.

And that Charlene and Florence MacFadden were guilty of illegally using spells to win.

"Yes!" Hilda jumped out of her seat. "Vindicated after all these years!"

"Hey!" Salem perked up. "Since Charlene won't be gloating about beating Hilda anymore, can we go to the Other Realm All-You-Can-Eat Clambake this year?"

"I don't know, Salem." Zelda frowned. "I'd still have to listen to Florence brag about beating me."

"Not if you wear earplugs," Salem suggested.

Sabrina glanced toward the judges' table as Drell and the other witches on the panel conferred.

After several long seconds, Drell stood up. He paused for dramatic effect, then boomed, "Pass!"

Thunderous applause and cheers filled the theater as Sabrina returned to her side of the stage. She took a deep breath and tried to relax as Agatha stepped forward. The competition wasn't over yet. She and the MacFadden girl would continue casting spells until one of them won a round.

Drell reached into a ceremonial cauldron on the table and pulled out a folded paper. He opened it, cleared his throat, then announced, "A spying eye spell."

A murmur of anticipation rippled through the audience.

Sabrina felt a rush of elation. Spy spells were tricky and subject to strange interpretations if the incantation wasn't worded exactly right. She crossed her fingers. A Spellman victory might be only one bad rhyme away.

Agatha paused to compose herself. She closed her eyes and took several deep breaths. When the tension drained from her face, she opened her eyes and focused—on Salem!

Sabrina fumed. The girl had deliberately targeted the cat to get back at her! The spell would be reversed when the contest was over, but zapping a helpless animal was pretty low.

Agatha's smug smile was firmly in place as she held her finger at the ready.

> *"Cloak and dagger, seek and hide,*
> *be my spying ears and eyes!"*

"What?" Salem cringed when Agatha zapped him. He immediately began to fade. Within seconds he was invisible except for his eyes, ears, and a huge, toothy grin with a brilliant *ping!*

"No offense, Salem, but I don't think that's a winning smile," Hilda said.

Sabrina tensed as the judges put their heads together. She wanted the competition to end so she could get back to her mortal life in Westbridge.

But I want to go home a winner! Sabrina had resented the unintended pressure her aunts had put on her to enter the Spelling Bee and restore the family's reputation; but now that she had met the Mac-Faddens, she was just as anxious for a Spellman victory as they were.

When Drell rose again, everyone leaned forward expectantly. "After due consideration, the judges unanimously rule that a *pinging* grin is hardly appropriate in an effective surreptitious surveillance spell."

"A what spell?" Florence asked, puzzled.

"An undercover spying spell that works," Zelda quietly explained.

Drell scowled at the whispering witches, then continued. "Therefore, Agatha MacFadden's spell fails and Sabrina Spellman is declared this year's winner!"

"Wahoo!" Sabrina raised victorious fists and jumped with joy.

More cheers and whistles erupted from the audience.

"I'd giggle with glee, but my teeth seem to be stuck," Salem muttered. He slowly returned to normal along with the other subjects as the effects of the contest spells wore off.

Hilda and Zelda grabbed each other and laughed. "She won! She won!"

Agatha glowered at Sabrina, then stalked into the wings.

Florence and Charlene sat in frozen, dumbstruck disbelief.

Drell picked up an envelope and motioned Sabrina to join him in the center of the stage.

"Gosh, I hope it's a gift certificate to WitchWare on-line," Hilda said. "We could upgrade the laptop."

"Good idea!" Zelda grinned, then became more subdued. "But it's Sabrina's prize and she can use whatever it is for whatever she wants."

"Like keeping the adorable family cat in caviar and fresh shrimp for the next six months," Salem sighed.

Sabrina hurried to join the head of the Witches' Council in the spotlight. She had tried hard to win so the MacFaddens would stop taunting her aunts. She hadn't thought about actually winning *something*. But since first prize might be a lifetime subscription to *Other Realm Geographic* or a shopping spree at Novelty Potions and Spells, she didn't have any trouble containing her excitement.

"Congratulations, Sabrina." Drell smiled like he actually meant it. "As this year's winner your name will, of course, be engraved on the permanent plaque at the base of the mountain."

"Cool!" Sabrina tried to look suitably impressed. "What did I win?"

"Oh, yes." Drell pushed a lock of hair back under his hat. "And I'm pleased to present you with"— Sabrina held her breath as Drell opened the envelope—"a reality check!" Drell waved a small, imprinted paper, then gave it to Sabrina.

The audience oohed and ahhed.

"That should have been mine!" Furious, Agatha stormed toward her aunts.

"Don't worry, Agatha." Florence put a comforting arm around the pouting girl's shoulders, then turned to her sister. "We'll get even."

Charlene's flaming red curls bounced as she nodded. "Soon."

Sabrina stared at the check. Her name magically appeared on the Payable To line in gleaming gold script. There weren't any spaces for a cash value. "What is *this?*"

"A reality check. *Don't* ask me to say it again." Shaking his head, Drell pulled off his pointed wizard hat and left as the house lights came up.

"I don't *need* to check my reality! I live in the mortal world with a talking cat and two eccentric witches!" Sabrina slumped with disappointment.

Drell just kept walking.

"You're a big help," Sabrina muttered. Her aunts and Salem rushed over as she hopped off the stage.

"You were great, Sabrina!" Hilda took the check from her niece's hand. "And this is fantastic! I don't think they've ever awarded a reality check before."

"We should probably put it in the safe deposit box and save it for an emergency," Zelda said.

"I think she should cash it in now," Salem purred. "I'm sure we can figure out exactly what point in time the Other Realm cops figured out I was trying to take over the world. With a little more security, I would have gotten away with it. Then I wouldn't be a cat."

"Wait a minute." Sabrina looked from one aunt to the other. "I'm obviously out of the loop here. What exactly *is* a reality check?"

"Very rare." Hilda handed the check back with a wistful sigh. "The Witches' Council is the only institution with the power to issue them and they don't do it very often."

"That didn't answer my question," Sabrina said. "What can *I* do with it?"

"After you endorse it, you can cash it in to change *one* instance of reality without any dire repercussions." Zelda smiled, but her tone was grave.

"What's the catch?" Sabrina asked. She had been a witch long enough to know that anything magical that seemed too good to be true usually was. She was certain the reality check was no exception.

"No catch," Zelda assured her. "That's why I think you should save it for an unexpected disaster."

"She shouldn't have it at all!" Florence marched forward, flanked by Charlene and Agatha. They stopped in a line to confront the Spellmans. Pointing fingers twitched at their sides.

"Sabrina won fair and square," Zelda huffed.

"Which is more than *you* can say!" Hilda fixed Charlene with a scathing scowl.

"So now we're even and maybe we can all be friends, right?" Still basking in the glow of victory, Sabrina wasn't in the mood to feud. She looked hopefully at Agatha, but the girl stubbornly folded her arms and frowned.

Charlene planted her hands on her hips to square off with Hilda. "Just because I outsmarted you doesn't mean you're a better witch than I am, Hilda Spellman."

"Oh, yeah?" Hilda's eyes narrowed. "Maybe we should step outside and have this out once and for all."

"No need for that," Florence said.

"Really?" A storm brewed under Zelda's calm exterior. "Then you *admit* you put a verbal dyslexia spell on me to win the Spelling Bee, Florence?"

"Never!" Florence stiffened.

"I guess a truce isn't an option then?" Sabrina asked even though no one was listening. She didn't blame Aunt Hilda and Aunt Zelda for being upset, but the confrontation was quickly stripping the luster off her winning glow. "So how about a cold war strategy? You know, where nobody on one side speaks to anyone on the other side."

"Yes, I'm tired of talking." Florence's eyes blazed.

"Me, too!" Charlene rolled up her sleeves.

"So are we." Zelda picked up Salem and took Hilda's arm. "Come on, Sabrina. We're leaving."

As Sabrina turned to follow her aunts, Charlene began an incantation.

> *"Two and four and time to do,*
> *Hilda, now the laugh's on you!"*

Charlene whipped off a point, catching Hilda totally off-guard.

Hilda began to giggle.

Florence picked up the chant.

*"Two and four, not over yet,
here and there she will forget!"*

Zelda flinched when Florence pointed at her.

"Hey!" Sabrina quickly pointed a protective ward around herself when Agatha raised her finger. She didn't know what the nasty little witch had in mind, but it wouldn't be pleasant. Sabrina rejected her own inclination to turn Agatha into a bunch of sour grapes.

Furious because Sabrina had blocked her, Agatha clenched her fists and stamped her foot.

Safe from the girl's witchy whims, Sabrina turned her attention back to her aunts. They hadn't been as lucky. Florence and Charlene had blind-sided them before they could defend themselves.

Hilda doubled over with hysterical laughter.

Zelda blinked at the cat cradled in her arms. "What a pretty kitty. Are you lost?"

"No," Salem drawled. "I'm right here."

"Aunt Zelda?" When her aunt didn't respond, Sabrina touched her arm. "Hello? Aunt Zelda?"

Hilda collapsed on the floor, still laughing.

"Hmmm?" Zelda looked up at Sabrina, her expression blank. "Do I know you?"

Oh, boy! Sabrina stared, numb with shock. Aunt Zelda didn't recognize her, and Aunt Hilda was rolling on the floor, laughing so hard she couldn't catch her breath.

"Are you lost?" Aunt Zelda asked Sabrina.

"Lost would seem to be the operative word," Salem said. "As in you've totally lost it."

Zelda frowned at the cat. "Do I know you?"

Think! Sabrina forced herself to remain calm. Living with eccentric aunts who were also witches' was one thing. She was not up to coping with eccentric witch aunts who had been turned into an airhead and a hysteric.

Sabrina looked at the reality check she still had clutched in her hand. If what her aunts had told her about the rare prize was true, she could cash it right now. Then Aunt Zelda and Aunt Hilda could counter the MacFaddens' ambush *before* the insidious spells hit.

Except Sabrina was certain there had to be a catch to the "no dire consequences" clause. The Witches' Council was extremely diligent about keeping the past intact. She had been incredibly fortunate that Drell had granted her request to turn back time so she could repeat her first day at Westbridge High. That had worked out great, but what if she changed an event, and the future that unfolded was *worse* than it would have been if she had left things alone?

Sabrina looked into Aunt Zelda's vacant eyes. Aunt Hilda was clutching her stomach and pounding on the floor, still laughing.

Cashing the check was tempting, but risky.

Sabrina stuffed it in her pocket.

Chapter 12

Sabrina spun to face the MacFaddens, and she opened her mouth to demand that they undo the spells on her aunts. She faltered, stricken with a sudden sense of déjà vu. She hesitated, overwhelmed by the unusually powerful feeling that she had done all this before.

Agatha was still glowering at her and pouting. "You are going to be *so* sorry you won this Spelling Bee, Sabrina."

Florence and Charlene nodded.

Behind her, Aunt Hilda gulped air between guffaws.

"Get over it, Agatha." Sabrina rolled her eyes. There was nothing worse than a sore loser, except a gloating winner. She flinched when Florence and Charlene turned their bold stares on her.

Aunt Zelda stepped up with Salem nestled in her arms. She smiled inanely at the MacFadden sisters. "Hello. Do I know you? My name is—" She paused, tilted her head, and froze when her brain failed to provide *any* information.

"Zelda," Salem said with exaggerated slowness. "Your name is Zel-da."

Zelda tilted her head the other way and patted the cat. "Hi, kitty."

"Brilliant spell, Florence. Zelda was always *so* insufferable about her superior intellect." Charlene smiled smugly. "And now she doesn't have one."

"And I just adore your sense of humor, Charlene." Florence cackled and pointed at Hilda.

"Okay, that's it!" Sabrina's smoldering eyes bore into the two women. "Reverse those spells. Right now."

"My, aren't *we* testy," Charlene huffed.

"Not a chance." Florence stubbornly lifted her chin.

"Told you you'd be sorry," Agatha smirked.

Now what? Sabrina's stare hardened even though her insides turned to nervous mush. The Spelling Bee had proven she was a better witch than Agatha, but she couldn't out-witch all three MacFaddens if they pooled their magic and ganged up on her.

When in doubt, bluff!

Sabrina pulled the reality check out of her pocket. She was sure it was a time bomb, and she had no intention of cashing it, but the MacFaddens didn't know that. "How does this thing work, Salem?"

"I thought you'd never ask," the cat said. "Just endorse the back and write down what you want to change under your signature."

"Got a pen?" Sabrina held out her hand.

The cat patted his black fur with his paw. "No," he drawled sarcastically.

"Wait a minute." Sabrina opened the purse dangling from Aunt Zelda's arm and pulled out a pen.

"All right! We'll cancel the spells." Scowling, Charlene waved her hand. She exhaled with disgust and flounced away.

"Spoilsport." Florence flicked a casual point over her shoulder as she grabbed Agatha's arm and followed Charlene.

Agatha looked back and smiled.

That was way too easy, Sabrina thought as the defeated MacFadden family marched up the theater aisle conferring in whispers.

"What are you doing on the floor, Hilda?" Zelda asked.

Distracted by her recovering aunts, Sabrina put the vindictive MacFaddens out of her mind. At least their spells had been reversed, although Aunt Zelda apparently had no memory of her memory lapse. On the other hand, Aunt Hilda was very much aware of the MacFaddens' foul play.

"Plotting my revenge against Charlene," Hilda groaned as she got to her feet.

"Stooping to her level won't solve anything. Besides, now that Sabrina's won the Spelling Bee, I don't think they'll be bothering us again." Zelda scratched Salem behind the ears.

"I'm not so sure about that." Salem's tail twitched with agitation.

"Neither am I." Sabrina's thoughts turned back to the MacFaddens as she followed her aunts toward the amphitheater lobby. They were obnoxious, sneaky, and bent on revenge.

She didn't trust them.

As Hilda stepped into the feeder tube that connected to the mortal world transit hub, Sabrina stopped dead. "Wait!"

Zelda hung back while Hilda was whisked away in the transparent tube. "What is it, Sabrina? Did you forget something?"

Sabrina frowned. She *felt* like she had forgotten something, but that wasn't what was bothering her. She pulled the rumpled reality check out of her pocket as the tube brought Aunt Hilda back.

"Did I miss anything?" Hilda asked as she stepped back into the lobby.

"No, but I can't shake the feeling that I have." Sabrina shook her head, then shrugged. "You've known the MacFaddens for a long time, right?"

"Much too long," Zelda said.

"I'd be happy if we'd never met," Hilda added. "Why? Aside from the obvious."

"Well, don't you think it's suspicious that they removed the spells without putting up much of a fight?"

"I do," Salem said.

"What spells?" Zelda frowned, bewildered.

"I'll explain later." Hilda patted Zelda's arm, then glanced at Sabrina. "Now that you mention it, yes. Charlene and Florence are like bulldogs with a bone when it comes to getting and keeping the upper hand. They don't let go or give up."

"Exactly. Agatha, too," Sabrina sighed, then held up the reality check. "Honestly now, what's the downside of cashing this reality check?"

"There isn't one," Zelda said.

"Except for the possibility of a repeating time loop." Hilda shrugged. "And that only happens when the person going back to change something doesn't follow through."

"But that's a rare occurrence," Zelda explained. "Whoever cashes a reality check remembers *everything* until the instant *after* the designated event-moment passes."

"Really?" Sabrina brightened. Apparently, her fears about the reality check were unfounded. After all, it would be totally lame for the Witches' Council to award a first prize that wasn't worth anything. And she obviously hadn't cashed a reality check before or the MacFaddens' spells wouldn't have taken her aunts by surprise. "Got a pen?"

WHOOOSSHHHHHH!
Sabrina swayed slightly as the time-ripple de-

posited her in the past a few minutes before the event she had noted on the reality check. She was standing in front of the stage with her aunts just as she had been after she had won the Spelling Bee in the last reality. She listened as her aunts explained the reality check to her, but now she was well aware of how it worked. *Too cool!*

"No catch," Zelda assured her. "That's why I think you should save it for an unexpected disaster."

Sabrina blinked. In this reality, she still had the reality check clutched in her hand! *This* one could go in the bank.

"*She* shouldn't have it at all!" Right on cue, Florence MacFadden marched forward, flanked by Charlene and Agatha. They stopped in a line to confront the Spellmans with eyes narrowed.

Sabrina noted the fingers twitching at their sides and smiled.

"Sabrina won fair and square," Zelda huffed.

"Which is more than *you* can say!" Hilda fixed Charlene with a scathing scowl.

Charlene planted her hands on her hips to square off with Hilda. "Just because I outsmarted you doesn't mean you're a better witch than I am, Hilda Spellman."

"Oh, yeah?" Hilda's eyes narrowed. "Maybe we should step outside and have this out once and for all."

"No need for that," Florence said.

Sabrina tensed, mentally preparing for the imminent arrival of the event-moment.

"Really?" A storm brewed under Zelda's calm exterior. "Then you *admit* you put a verbal dyslexia spell on me to win the Spelling Bee, Florence?"

"Never!" Florence stiffened.

Charlene rolled up her sleeves.

"Come on, Sabrina." Zelda picked up Salem and took Hilda's arm. "We're leaving."

This time when Sabrina turned to follow her aunts, she muttered under her breath with her pointing finger ready.

> *"Shield I spin don't just protect,*
> *any spell that hits reflect."*

Sabrina twirled her pointing finger to encompass her aunts and herself.

Feeling dizzy, Sabrina staggered a little and glanced back when she heard Charlene's nasal voice drone an incantation.

> *"Two and four and time to do,*
> *Hilda, now the laugh's on you!"*

Charlene whipped off a point at Hilda.

Hilda flinched, then frowned when Florence picked up the chant.

*"Two and four, not over yet,
here and there she will forget!"*

Zelda blinked as Florence's finger targeted her.

A protective ward that had mysteriously formed around Sabrina and her aunts twanged as the Mac-Faddens' spells impacted. Multicolored lights swirled across the transparent shield, then coalesced into two streams of light that zipped around the invisible cylinder in opposite directions.

"Where'd this shield come from?" Hilda tentatively poked it with her finger.

Sabrina glanced at the reality check in her hand. She must have cashed in a previous check. Nothing else explained the presence of the ward.

"I don't know, but I'm glad it's here." Zelda nodded toward the MacFaddens. "Look."

Agatha's petulant scowl changed into a puzzled frown.

Charlene and Florence backed away with stricken expressions as the two streams of colored light shot out of the shield like bolts of lightning. The women screamed and ducked, but they couldn't escape their own reflected magic. The bolts dissipated, bathing them in rainbow light.

Charlene giggled, then snickered, then burst out laughing.

"Well, Charlene's getting the last laugh, as usual," Salem chuckled.

Agatha ran up to the short, chubby woman. "What's wrong, Aunt Charlene? This isn't funny."

Charlene laughed and laughed.

Agatha grabbed onto Florence. "Do something, Aunt Florence!"

"Do I know you?" Florence smiled.

"What did you do to my aunts?" Agatha demanded.

"Looks to me like they just got a taste of their own medicine," Hilda grinned.

"I wonder how?" Zelda cast a questioning glance at Sabrina.

Sabrina shrugged and waved her finger. The protective shield dissipated. "Time to go!"

"I'm ready." Hilda led the way up the aisle.

"Me, too. I'm exhausted after watching Sabrina cast all those spells." Zelda beamed at Sabrina. "But I'm so proud of you. You won the Spelling Bee *and* saved us from the MacFaddens' horrible spells."

"How'd you do that?" Salem asked.

"Apparently, I used one of these." Sabrina waved the reality check. "I've got a question."

Aunt Zelda settled Salem into the crook of one arm and hugged Sabrina around the shoulders with the other. "Don't worry. The reality check is perfectly harmless."

"Even though I can use it over and over again?" Sabrina had been a witch long enough to know that anything magic that seemed too good to be true usually was. She was sure the reality check was no exception.

"Only until you change something so you don't win it in the first place," Zelda explained.

"But please, don't do that!" Hilda shuddered. "Aside from not wanting you to lose the Spelling Bee to a MacFadden, can you imagine what the world would be like if *Agatha* had a reality check?"

"I'd rather not. The mere thought sets my teeth on edge." Salem tucked his head under Zelda's arm.

"Chaos would reign," Zelda said. "Even prudent people get careless when they know that the consequences of any decision can be changed."

Sabrina sighed as they paused in the lobby to wait for the feeder tube. Maybe the check wasn't as harmless as Aunt Zelda thought. She had already used it once—that she knew of. Turning the Mac-Faddens' spells back on them had been worth it, but she *was* a teenager. Knowing she could alter the past whenever something went wrong would influence *every* decision she made. She wouldn't be able to resist the temptation to use the reality check again.

And again and again.

"When we get home, I think we should go out and celebrate Sabrina's victory," Zelda said as they all piled into the tube.

"I thought you were exhausted." Hilda pressed the button for the central transport hub to the mortal world.

"Not that tired!" Zelda laughed.

"Pizza or Chinese?" Hilda asked.

"I know this great sushi place," Salem said.

"I'm open." Smiling, Sabrina held up the reality check and tore it into tiny pieces. Being able to fix her mistakes with a signature would take all the fun out of getting into trouble.

Her aunts nodded their approval.

"No!" Salem wailed. "That's my ticket out of this fur coat!"

"Lighten up, Salem!" Sabrina tossed the check pieces in the air. "Let's party!"

About the Author

DIANA G. GALLAGHER lives in Florida with her husband, Marty Burke, three dogs, three cats, and a cranky parrot. Before becoming a full-time writer, she made her living in a variety of occupations, including hunter seat equitation instructor, folk musician, and fantasy artist. Best known for her hand-colored prints depicting the doglike activities of *Woof: The House Dragon,* she won a Hugo for Best Fan Artist in 1988.

Her first science fiction novel, *The Alien Dark,* was published in 1990. Since then, she has written novels for all age groups in multiple series for Minstrel Books. These include Star Trek for young adults, The Secret World of Alex Mack, Are You Afraid of the Dark, The Mystery Files of Shelby Woo, and Sabrina, the Teenage Witch. Her first (adult) Buffy the Vampire Slayer novel, *Obsidian Fate,* appeared in September 1999. Two additional Buffy novels, *Prime Evil* and *Doomsday Deck,* are scheduled for spring and fall of 2000.